A Note from Stephanie about Becoming a Winning Loser

Ready, set, serve! A tennis expert I am *not*. So, why am I about to play against Darcy, my best friend, in the most important tennis game of my life? Beats me! I guess I got sort of jealous when Darcy started paying attention to Sara Albright. Sara's new at school, and a terrific tennis player. Before I knew it, I had challenged Darcy and Sara to a doubles match—in front of the whole school!

The only trouble is, I'm not sure I want to win. Because if I do, Darcy may never speak to me again! Doesn't that sound more like losing than winning?

It may take me some time to figure out the answer. In the meantime, let me tell you about the people who helped me get into top tennis-playing condition—my family. My unusual family.

Right now there are nine people and a dog living in our house—and for all I know, someone new could move in at any time. There's me, my big sister, D.J., my little sister, Michelle, and my dad, Danny. But that's just the beginning.

When my mom died, Dad needed help. So he asked his old college buddy, Joey Gladstone, and my uncle Jesse to come live with us, to help take care of me and my sisters.

Back then, Uncle Jesse didn't know much about taking care of three little girls. He was more into rock 'n' roll. Joey didn't know anything about kids either—but it sure was funny watching him learn!

Having Uncle Jesse and Joey around was like having three dads instead of one! But then something even better happened—Uncle Jesse fell in love. He married Rebecca Donaldson, Dad's cohost on his TV show, *Wake Up, San Francisco*. Aunt Becky's so nice—she's more like a big sister than an aunt.

Next Uncle Jesse and Aunt Becky had twin baby boys. Their names are Nicky and Alex, and they are adorable!

I love being part of a big family. Still, things can get pretty crazy when you live in such a full house!

FULL HOUSE™: Stephanie novels

Available from MINSTREL Books

FULL HOUSE™
Stephanie

Doubles or Nothing

Eliza West

A Parachute Press Book

Published by POCKET BOOKS
New York   London   Toronto   Sydney   Tokyo   Singapore

A MINSTREL PAPERBACK *Original*

A Minstrel Book published by
POCKET BOOKS, a division of Simon & Schuster Inc.
1230 Avenue of the Americas, New York, NY 10020

A PARACHUTE PRESS BOOK

READING Copyright © and ™ 1996 by Warner Bros.

FULL HOUSE, characters, names and all related indicia are trademarks of Warner Bros. © 1996.

ISBN: 0-671-56841-8

First Minstrel Books printing August 1996

10 9 8 7 6 5 4 3 2 1

A MINSTREL BOOK and colophon are registered trademarks of Simon & Schuster Inc.

Cover photo by Schultz Photography

Printed in the U.S.A.

Doubles or Nothing

CHAPTER
1

◆ ◢ ◣ ◆

"Where *is* that other tennis shoe?" Stephanie Tanner rummaged through her locker. "I know it's in here somewhere," she said.

Stephanie pushed her long blond hair behind her ears. She stared at her locker in disgust.

Darcy Powell and Allie Taylor, Stephanie's two best friends, exchanged glances.

"Here we go again," Allie said.

Allie had been Stephanie's best friend since kindergarten. She had wavy, light brown hair and green eyes. Allie was kind of quiet—especially around boys! But she and Stephanie had lots in common. They both loved music, reading, and funny movies.

"Face it, Stephanie," Allie added. "Your locker

is like a black hole. Things are always disappearing in it."

"I think it's more like a lost and found—for the whole school," Darcy joked.

Darcy was tall and slim. She often wore silver bangle bracelets that gleamed against her dark skin. She had brown hair and sparkling brown eyes. She was full of energy and had a great sense of humor. Darcy had been best friends with Stephanie and Allie since sixth grade.

Allie nudged Darcy. "Speaking of the lost and found, didn't you lose your blue sunglasses, Darcy?" she asked. "Because I think you just found them."

Darcy peered into Stephanie's locker. Her sunglasses were crammed onto the locker shelf under a pile of notebooks.

"Yes!" Darcy cried. She dug out the sunglasses and put them on. She checked her reflection in the mirror on the inside of the door.

"I've been looking everywhere for these," Darcy said. "How long have they been in your locker, Steph?"

"Beats me," Stephanie said. "But I still can't find my tennis shoe."

"Well, just wear your cross-trainers," Darcy suggested.

"These?" Stephanie glanced down at the sneakers she'd worn to school that day. "Do you think they're good enough for tennis?" she asked. "I mean, this is the first Girls Tennis Club meeting of the year. I want to make sure I'm dressed right."

"Don't worry," Allie told her. She held up a piece of paper. "Here's the flyer for Try-a-Club Month. It says you don't need to bring equipment to the first meeting. That's the way it is every year."

"But what does it say about the Girls Tennis Club?" Stephanie asked.

"Just that anyone interested should meet in the gym at three-thirty," Allie said.

"Well, I brought my own racket." Darcy pointed to her gym bag on the floor. "It's brand new. Strings as tight as a drum and a great sweet spot."

"What's a sweet spot?" Allie asked.

"I hope it's a place you go after a match, to eat ice cream and sodas," Stephanie teased.

"No way," Darcy said with a laugh. "It means the place on the racket where you're supposed to hit the ball."

"How did you know that?" Stephanie asked.

"I took a tennis lesson at my parents' tennis club this weekend," Darcy said. "You know, to get ready."

3

"Wow. I hope everyone in the club isn't as serious about tennis as that," Stephanie said.

"Don't you want to get better?" Darcy asked. "I do."

"Sure," Stephanie said. "But I also want to have fun."

"This club will be tons of fun," Darcy assured her. "Especially with the three of us playing together!"

"Yeah, that'll make it a major blast!" Stephanie agreed.

Allie twisted her hair around her finger. She glanced down at the flyer in her hand. "Uh, you know, there are lots of great clubs to try this month," she said.

"Sure," Darcy said. "But I'm totally psyched about Girls Tennis Club."

"Me too. Last night I even hit some balls against the side of the garage, just to try things out," Stephanie said.

"How did you do?" Darcy asked.

"Not so great," Stephanie admitted. "But I was using my dad's old racket. And I don't think it even *has* a sweet spot!"

Darcy and Stephanie burst out laughing. Allie gave them a weak grin.

"Aren't you psyched too?" Stephanie asked Allie.

"Sure. I mean, maybe," Allie answered. She shifted her eyes away.

"What do you mean, maybe?" Stephanie demanded. Darcy stared at Allie.

Allie hesitated. "Well, it's, um, it's just that I was thinking about trying the Guitar Club instead," she said. "It meets at the same time as the Girls Tennis Club, so I can't do both. And you know how much I love music. I could actually take guitar lessons for free!" Allie's eyes shone in excitement.

Stephanie gazed at Allie in surprise. "I didn't know you wanted to do that. You said you were joining tennis with us," she said.

"Yeah, this is the first I've heard about the Guitar Club," Darcy agreed.

"Well, I haven't *completely* decided yet," Allie admitted. "That's what Try-a-Club Month is all about, isn't it?" she asked.

"But, Allie, the Girls Tennis Club won't be the same without you," Darcy protested.

"Why didn't you tell us you were thinking of trying something else?" Stephanie asked.

"I tried to tell you last night," Allie explained.

5

"I wanted to do a three-way call with you and Darcy."

Allie had received the special phone hookup as a birthday gift from her parents. It let her speak to two people at once. It was a great arrangement for three best friends.

"So why didn't you call?" Stephanie asked her.

"I couldn't, Stephanie. Your line was busy forever. I finally gave up," Allie explained.

Stephanie groaned. "Tell me about it! Someone's *always* on the phone in my house!"

Stephanie's family was pretty unusual. Nine people lived in her house. Stephanie's older sister, D.J., was eighteen and in college. D.J. had just gotten her own phone line, but no one else was allowed to use it. That still left six people to share the family phone.

Besides Stephanie and her dad, there was Stephanie's younger sister, Michelle, who was nine. Then there were her uncle Jesse and his wife, Becky, who had an apartment in the attic of their house. And there was Joey Gladstone, her dad's best friend from college, who also lived with the family.

The only ones who didn't use the phone were Comet, the dog, and Stephanie's twin cousins. Alex and Nicky were only four. They didn't make phone

6

calls yet. But Stephanie knew that things would get even worse when they learned how to dial the phone!

"I'd give anything to have my own phone line, like you," Stephanie told Allie. "Even D.J. has her own line now," she complained.

"Enough about phone calls," Darcy interrupted. "What are you going to do about the Girls Tennis Club?"

"I'm not sure what to do," Allie said. "Why don't you guys just go ahead without me?"

"We can't do that," Stephanie protested. "We always do everything together."

"It wouldn't be the same without you," Darcy agreed.

"Best friends always stick together," Stephanie added.

"But I'm not sure I like tennis," Allie said.

"What's not to like?" Darcy asked. "We'll all share a court. It'll be major fun."

"Allie, I think guitar lessons would be really cool. But tennis is cool too. And the three of us can do that *together*," Stephanie argued.

"Well, why not try the Girls Tennis Club today and see if you like it?" Darcy suggested.

"Sure! You can try the Guitar Club next week.

Don't forget that you have this whole month to make up your mind. Please?" Stephanie begged.

"Yeah, just give it a try," Darcy urged.

'I don't know," Allie said.

Stephanie checked her watch. "Well, you'd better decide fast," she said. "Because the tennis meeting starts in exactly twelve minutes!"

CHAPTER
2

◆ ◀ ◆ ◆

"Okay," Allie said. "I'll do it. I'll try the Girls Tennis Club today."

"All right!" Stephanie cheered. "We'll be a winning team!"

"Allie, you made the right choice. You won't be sorry," Darcy added. She grabbed her gym bag. "Let's go, guys! I'm ready to rally!" Darcy raced down the hall.

Stephanie slammed her locker. She and Allie ran to catch up with Darcy.

"How am I supposed to keep up with her on the tennis court?" Allie asked. "I can't even keep up with her in the halls!"

"Don't worry, Allie," Stephanie said. "Tennis Club won't be nearly this hard!"

They had barely enough time to change into shorts and T-shirts in the locker room. By the time Stephanie, Darcy, and Allie hurried into the gym, the rest of the group was already heading outside to the tennis courts.

They joined the back of the crowd and gathered around the courts which were alongside the football field. Stephanie recognized most of the girls in the group.

Gwenith Gilmour caught Stephanie's eye and nodded. "Hey, Stephanie," she called.

Gwenith was a short girl with long bouncy brown curls. She and Stephanie were in the same grade but they didn't share any classes this year. They used to have study hall together in seventh grade. Gwenith was a lot of fun, Stephanie remembered.

"Hi, Gwenith," Stephanie said. "Study hall isn't the same without you."

"I know," Gwenith joked. "Since you're not around, I actually have to study!"

Stephanie laughed. "I like your outfit." she said. Gwenith was wearing a bright blue short-sleeved T-shirt. The shirt exactly matched a pair of baggy shorts. The shorts tied with a drawstring around the waist.

"Oh, thanks. I just bought it this weekend,"

Gwenith said. "It's been a long time since I played tennis. I didn't have a thing that fit me anymore." Gwenith blushed. "I'm pretty much out of shape," she admitted.

"Well, it should be fun getting back *into* shape here," Stephanie told her.

"Yeah. I hope so." Gwenith smiled.

A sharp voice rang out behind Stephanie. "Excuse me, but you're not in the Girls Tennis Club, are you?"

Stephanie turned around. A tall girl with short blond hair stood behind her. She carried a zippered tennis case. Her name was embroidered across the cover: Sara Albright.

"Sure, this is the Girls Tennis Club," Stephanie said. "Hi, Sara. You're new at John Muir Middle School, aren't you? I'm Stephanie and this is Gwenith."

"Oh. Hi." Sara smiled politely. "I wasn't sure this was the right place," she said. She gazed at Stephanie and Gwenith. "I guess you don't care what you wear," she said.

"Well, sure, we care," Stephanie said.

"I mean, this club obviously doesn't have rules about proper tennis attire," Sara explained.

"Don't we look right?" Gwenith asked. She pulled at the waist of her shorts and blushed again.

Stephanie tucked her bright pink T-shirt into her cutoff shorts, feeling suddenly self-conscious.

Sara raised an eyebrow. She was wearing a white tennis dress. It zipped up the front and had a crisply pleated skirt. It looked trendy and professional at the same time.

She also wore light blue terry-cloth sweatbands around her wrists and a matching sweatband around her forehead. Her tennis sneakers were the fanciest Stephanie had ever seen. Plus, they were absolutely spotless.

"Well, it's only our first meeting," Stephanie said. "You weren't supposed to dress up. Or even bring your own equipment," she added, laughing lightly.

"Well, they wouldn't allow such casual clothing at my old school," Sara said.

Stephanie shrugged.

"Who's in charge here anyway?" Sara asked.

"Ms. Spano," Gwenith told her. "She's the gym teacher."

"And a great tennis coach," Stephanie added, even though she'd never had Ms. Spano for tennis before.

Sara stared at Ms. Spano, who stood talking with a group of girls. The teacher also wore a sweatband across her forehead, but she was wearing a pair of loose-fitting shorts and an old, faded polo shirt. Sara hurried toward her.

"I wonder if Sara thinks Ms. Spano is in proper tennis attire?" Gwenith joked. Stephanie laughed.

Allie and Darcy hurried over to them.

"Wasn't that Sara Albright?" Allie asked Stephanie.

"She's new in school," Darcy added. "She's been here for only three weeks and she acts as if she owns the place."

"I believe that," Stephanie murmured.

Gwenith giggled.

"So, what's Sara like?" Allie asked.

"Yeah. Is she a snob, like everyone says?" Darcy said.

"I don't know. But she seems very big on rules," Stephanie said.

Ms. Spano clapped her hands for attention. "Okay, girls, quiet down and gather around." Ms. Spano sat on the ground and waited while everyone sat in a circle around her.

"See you later," Gwenith told Stephanie. She joined the group sitting closest to Ms. Spano. Stephanie, Darcy, and Allie sat a little way behind the crowd so they could talk together.

"First, we'll go over some of the club rules," Ms. Spano said.

Stephanie nudged Allie. "Sara should like that," she whispered. Allie and Darcy giggled.

Ms. Spano glanced down at some notes she had on a clipboard. "Well, I had a whole speech written out. But speeches are really too formal," she began. "So, I'll just say what I feel." She gave the group a big smile.

"I'm really glad to see such a big turnout for this first Girls Tennis Club meeting," she continued. "I love tennis. It's my favorite sport. And after you've tried the club, I hope tennis will be your favorite too."

Stephanie grinned at Darcy and Allie. *This is going to be so much fun*, she thought to herself. *I like Ms. Spano already!*

"I'm sure you all have different backgrounds and tennis experience," the teacher continued. "That's fine. Every level of play has its own challenges. And we can all learn from one another," she said.

"I like her attitude," Darcy whispered.

"Me too," Allie agreed.

Sara Albright raised her hand. "What about proper attire? And the right equipment?" she asked.

Ms. Spano smiled. "Anyone can use the school's rackets. I'll try to help you choose a size and weight that's right for you," she said.

14

"But isn't it much better to have your own racket?" Laura Bracken asked.

"Sure, it's ideal to have a racket that's perfect for you. And if you already have one, great." Ms. Spano nodded toward Sara's racket case in approval. "But don't worry about equipment yet. The important thing is to learn the game, and learn it right," she finished.

"I'm glad she said that," Allie whispered. "I'd hate to buy a racket and find out I'm no good at this."

Sara raised her hand again. "What about ranking players?" she asked. "To make sure we have the right partners, I mean."

"We'll get to that," Ms. Spano said. "In fact, we'll be working on our doubles strategy soon."

"How soon?" Sara called out.

"Next week, I hope," the teacher answered. "We'll form doubles teams and challenge each other in a round robin tournament. But first, I want to see where everyone's game is, and help you feel comfortable on the courts. That's the way to learn to love tennis."

The teacher stood up and everyone stood with her.

"Okay. Choose a partner and pair up," Ms. Spano said. "Grab a racket and find a court. Rally first with your partner. Then we'll try a doubles game. And remember—have fun!"

There was a buzz of excited chatter as the girls leapt to their feet. Most of them grabbed rackets that belonged to the school. Darcy helped Stephanie and Allie choose rackets that were good for them. By the time they were done, the other girls were already pairing off and finding courts.

Allie grabbed Stephanie's sleeve. "Uh, Steph, we're supposed to pair up now. But there's *three* of us."

"Oh, that's okay," Stephanie said. "We'll take turns being partners."

"Sure. Nobody will care," Darcy assured Allie. "Ms. Spano said not to worry about the rules. We're supposed to have fun, remember?"

"And feel comfortable on the court," Allie added. "I'm for that."

"So, let's give it a try," Darcy said. "Come on. We can take that court in the corner. No one will bother us there."

"Yeah, let's go," Stephanie told Allie. "No one will mind three of us playing anyway."

They hurried to the far court. Stephanie and Allie stood on one side of the net. Darcy stood across from them.

"Allie, why don't you and I hit first?" Darcy suggested.

Stephanie stood to one side. Darcy bounced the ball and lobbed it over the net. Allie ran, swung at the ball—and missed.

"Too bad. Try again," Darcy called.

Allie tried, but she managed to return only two balls. Darcy frowned and shifted her racket from hand to hand in frustration.

"You'll do better soon," Stephanie told Allie. "How about the two of us playing against Darcy?" she asked.

"I'll try anything," Allie answered.

Stephanie took her place on the court next to Allie. Darcy hit the ball over the net and Stephanie ran toward it.

"Mine!" Stephanie called.

"Two against one?" a voice said. Stephanie glanced up in surprise. The ball bounced at her feet and rolled away.

Sara was standing on their court. "I never heard of playing doubles with *three* people," she said.

"Oh, well, the three of us are sort of a special team," Stephanie told her.

"Not anymore," Sara said. "Ms. Spano just told me to be your fourth player."

CHAPTER
3

◆ ◀ ▪ ◆

There was a moment of silence.

"Well, Sara, I guess you should stand next to Darcy, then," Stephanie finally said. "Okay, you guys?" She glanced at her friends.

Allie frowned. Darcy shrugged.

"Sure. I'm ready," Darcy replied.

"Me too," said Allie.

"Who wants to serve?" Stephanie asked.

"Not me," said Allie. "I don't know how."

"Then I'll start," Stephanie offered. She bounced the ball once or twice, then tossed it into the air. She drew back her racket and started to swing at the ball.

"Hold it!" Sara called out. "What are you doing?"

Stephanie was so startled, she totally missed the ball. "I'm serving," she told Sara.

Sara laughed. "That's not the right way to do it!" she said.

Stephanie glanced at Allie and Darcy. "Sure it is," Stephanie said. "I may not be a great tennis player, but I know how to serve."

"No, I mean, you didn't choose the server. You're not following professional procedure," Sara explained. "You know."

"Uh, sure, I know," Stephanie said. She shrugged, then turned toward Darcy and Allie, rolling her eyes. Her friends giggled.

"Funny," Sara said without cracking a smile. "This is how you decide who's going to serve."

Sara walked up to the net. "See—one side of the racket has the name printed on it. That's 'heads.' You spin the racket to find out who serves."

"I never heard that," Allie said.

"You obviously don't play much tennis," Sara replied.

Allie flushed red.

"It's just like flipping a coin," Sara explained. She spoke very carefully, as if she were talking to two-year-olds. "Whoever wins the call serves first."

"Well, I knew that," Darcy said. "But this isn't exactly a real tennis match."

"Yeah, we were just going to hit the ball for fun," Stephanie agreed.

"Well, that's the way it should be done," Sara said. "We might as well follow the rules, right?" Sara didn't wait for an answer. "Darcy and I can be a team. We'll call 'heads.'" Sara spun the racket.

"Heads it is!" Sara said. "My serve. Unless you want it, Darcy."

"That's okay," Darcy said.

The girls took their positions. Sara served to Stephanie. The ball whizzed over the net. Stephanie jumped back.

"What was that? A tennis ball or an unidentified flying object?" Stephanie said. She glanced at Allie and they both started laughing.

"Let's try again," Sara said.

She served. Somehow Stephanie managed to return the ball. Sara ran for the ball and whacked it back at Allie. Allie swung. Her racket whooshed through the air. The ball landed behind her.

"Sorry," Allie mumbled.

"Well, it's not your fault. You're only a beginner," Sara said. "Let's try again."

Sara sent another ball over the net. Allie and

Stephanie stood frozen as it whizzed between them.

Allie glanced at Stephanie. "I thought you'd get it," she said.

"I thought you would," Stephanie said.

They both started giggling.

"Come on, you two," Sara shouted. "Quit fooling around!"

"Are we having fun yet?" Allie muttered to Stephanie.

Stephanie rolled her eyes. "Not much," she whispered back.

"Let's go!" Sara called.

To Stephanie's surprise, they actually managed to keep the ball in play for a while. Then Allie's return slammed into the net.

"Fifteen to zero!" Sara shouted.

Stephanie blinked in surprise. "What are you doing? Who said anything about keeping score?"

"Well, of course we're keeping score," Sara replied. "What's the point in playing if we don't keep score?"

"It does make it more fun," Darcy said to Stephanie. "And we should all learn how to keep score too," she added.

"I guess so," Stephanie began. "But—"

"Okay, team! Listen up!" Ms. Spano called. Everyone stopped playing. Ms. Spano motioned them closer and they gathered around her again.

"Let's call it quits for the day," Ms. Spano said. "I've seen all of you in action now. At our next meeting we can work on your individual strengths—and weaknesses." She grinned.

Sara waved her hand in the air. "When can we start working on our doubles strategy?" she asked.

"At our next meeting," Ms. Spano answered.

"Great!" Sara said. "That will make practices more of a challenge. I like to think hard *and* play hard."

"Everyone who used a school racket, please return it to the box in the locker room. See you next time," Ms. Spano finished.

A group of girls gathered around the teacher to ask questions.

"Listen, I've got to run," Allie said to Stephanie. "My mom is probably out front in the car, waiting for me. We're going to my cousin's for dinner tonight."

"Wait, Allie! What did you think of the club?" Stephanie asked. "Are you joining or not?"

"Um, I'll call you tonight, Steph. We'll talk then," Allie answered.

"Yeah, talk to you later, Allie," Darcy called.

Allie hurried away. Stephanie turned to Darcy.

"Well, that was some meeting—" she began to say. Just then Sara walked by on her way to the locker room.

"Hey, Sara, you're a really good player," Darcy said to her.

"Thanks!" Sara replied. She slowed down and Darcy began walking beside her.

Stephanie followed after them.

"Your serve is awesome," Darcy continued. "You must play a lot."

"I do. I was on the tennis team at my old school," Sara told Darcy. "It wasn't a club like this, that anyone could join. You had to try out. It was very competitive."

"We don't have a real tennis team at John Muir," Darcy said.

"Really?" Sara seemed surprised. "I guess people here aren't really serious players, then."

"Well, some kids are, but not many," Darcy said.

"Maybe the best players could get together and play a few matches," Sara suggested.

"I guess that could be fun for them," Darcy said.

"I was including *you*, Darcy," Sara said. "You have a lot of potential."

"You think so?" Darcy smiled.

Stephanie pushed up next to Darcy. "Yeah," she

23

put in. "Darcy is the most athletic of all of us. She's a fantastic skier."

"Is she?" Sara asked. She turned to Darcy. "About how often do you play tennis?"

"Maybe a few times a month," Darcy said. "But I'd like to start playing more. How about you?"

"I used to play every day," Sara said.

"Sounds like a lot of work," Stephanie said.

"Well, I sort of *had* to work hard," Sara said. "I was the team captain."

"Really?" Darcy asked. "I'm impressed."

Sara nodded. "Yeah. It was a lot of responsibility. The team captain has to set an example for everybody else."

"I guess you're practically a tennis doubles expert," Stephanie said.

"Well, not really," Sara said. "I was a singles player."

"Most serious players don't bother with doubles," Darcy explained to Stephanie.

"Oh. Well, I think doubles is a lot more fun anyway," Stephanie replied. "You get to be with your friends, right, Darcy?"

"Yeah. But I'd like to learn more about playing singles sometime," Darcy said. "Sara, do you have any advice for me? I mean, even though we didn't play a real game today."

"We should work on your backhand," Sara answered. She hesitated. "And since you're asking for advice, you've all got to work on your footing. Especially you, Stephanie. You really should wear tennis shoes. Not those cross-trainers. Footing is very important."

Stephanie frowned. "They call them cross-trainers because they're good for *all* sports," she mumbled.

"I know. But the right equipment makes a difference," Sara said.

"*Your* tennis shoes are way cool," Darcy said to Sara. "I wish I could get a pair like them."

"You probably should. If you want to get serious, that is," Sara told her.

Why do we have to be so serious? Whatever happened to having fun? Stephanie said to herself.

They reached the locker room and stepped inside. Stephanie quickly changed out of her tennis clothes.

"Ready to go, Darce?" she asked.

"Sure." Darcy turned to Sara. "How are you getting home?"

"Oh, I'll walk," Sara said. "I live only a few blocks away from school. On Buena Vista Road. Do you know it?"

25

"Yeah. Hey, why don't Steph and I walk you home?" Darcy suggested.

"Do you really want to?" Sara asked.

"Sure," Darcy replied. "We walk that way lots of times instead of taking the late bus. Okay with you, Steph?" she asked.

"Well, I guess walking is a good way to cool down," Stephanie said.

"Yeah. And it'll be our way of saying welcome to John Muir Middle School," Darcy told Sara.

"Thanks!" Sara grabbed her tennis bag and smiled. "All set."

Darcy walked beside Sara as they left the school. They headed toward Buena Vista Road.

"You know, Sara, I should probably practice more days a week too. Because I really want to get better," Darcy said.

"We could meet an extra day or two after school. That would probably help your backhand," Sara said.

"My dad tried to help me already. He got me a special tennis lesson at our sports club," Darcy told her.

"Your family belongs to a club?" Sara asked. "Do they have good tennis facilities?"

Darcy nodded. "The best. Indoor and outdoor

courts. It's the Marina Health and Sports Club. You should check it out."

"I will! I bet my parents would love to join," Sara said. She stopped walking. "Well, here's my street," she told them.

"I'd like to find out more about that club, Darcy," Sara added. "Maybe I'll see you tomorrow in school."

"Okay," Darcy said. "Bye, Sara."

"Bye," Stephanie added.

Sara waved and hurried toward a white stucco house.

"Whew!" Stephanie said as soon as Sara was out of earshot. "I never met anyone so totally obsessed with tennis. And she's so serious! I don't think she laughed once all afternoon."

"But she's the best player in the club," Darcy replied. "We can really learn a lot from her."

"I don't know. I was kind of surprised when she kept score," Stephanie said. "Couldn't she have eased up a little? I mean, it's only a club, not a professional team."

"I know. But Ms. Spano can't spend a lot of time with each of us. Having Sara around is practically like having a personal trainer." Darcy's eyes shone in excitement.

"I didn't think we needed our own personal trainer," Stephanie said.

They reached the Tanners' street. Stephanie paused at the corner. "I'll call you tonight, Darcy," she said.

"Sara can definitely help me with my backhand," Darcy continued. "And my serve. And—"

"Bye, Darcy," Stephanie said again.

"I'll bet Sara knows tons about strategy too." Darcy paused suddenly and looked at Stephanie in surprise. "Hey, weren't you going to say goodbye?" Darcy asked.

Stephanie grinned. "I said, good-bye, Darcy."

"I didn't hear you," Darcy told her.

"I noticed that." Stephanie shook her head. "I'll call you tonight," she said. "And maybe we can talk about something *besides* tennis!"

CHAPTER
4

◆ ◀ ◆ ◆

Stephanie dumped her backpack inside the front hall of her house. She headed straight for the refrigerator. D.J. was already in the kitchen. She was helping their dad chop up vegetables for a huge salad.

"Hi, everybody," Stephanie called. She pulled a bottle of juice out of the refrigerator. "What's up?"

"We're getting an early start on dinner," Danny Tanner told her. He kissed Stephanie on the cheek.

Stephanie slipped off the denim jacket she was wearing and hung it over the back of her chair.

"So that's where my new jean jacket is!" D.J. frowned at Stephanie. "I've been looking all over for it. Where did you get it?"

"The hall closet," Stephanie said. "And you

29

know the rule—it's okay to borrow anything in the hall closet."

D.J. sighed. "I can see what's going to happen next week," she said. "The minute I leave for my field trip, everything I own is going to disappear."

"Only if it's in the hall closet," Stephanie joked.

"Well, at least do me a favor," D.J. asked. "Put my jacket back in my room before I leave."

"What kind of trip is this, Deej?" Stephanie poured herself a second glass of juice.

"It's a marine ecology field trip," D.J. explained. "My class is spending a whole week studying the shoreline. We're going south, down near Carmel. I can't wait!"

"Sounds like fun," Stephanie said.

"As much fun as your tennis club?" Joey Gladstone walked into the kitchen. "Did you have a volley good time?" he quipped.

Everyone groaned. Joey hosted a radio show at a local station with Stephanie's uncle Jesse. The show was called *The Rush Hour Renegades*. Joey and Jesse did interviews with famous guests and told funny stories.

Joey also told lots of jokes. Bad jokes. He was famous for his terrible puns.

"The club was okay," Stephanie said. "But Allie and I lost our match. This new girl totally destroyed us." Stephanie shrugged. "And it wasn't even supposed to be a serious game."

"Well, I hope you worked up a serious appetite," Danny said. "We're having your favorite spaghetti dinner." He turned to D.J. "How are you doing with those tomatoes for the sauce?"

"I'm chopping as fast as I can," D.J. said. "You could help, Stephanie."

Stephanie peeked into the living room. She was dying to talk to Allie about the Girls Tennis Club. But Allie wouldn't be home until after dinner. Anyway, Stephanie could see that Michelle was on the phone again.

"Sure. I'll help," Stephanie agreed. She grabbed a tomato and chopped away. Then she helped her dad mix up a salad dressing. Soon dinner was almost ready.

Stephanie peeked into the living room again.

"That's easy. Little Rock," she heard Michelle say into the phone. Then Michelle listened into the receiver.

Stephanie sighed. She lifted the lid off a big pot of water. "Almost boiling," she told her dad.

"When it boils, could you add the spaghetti?" Danny asked.

"Okay." Stephanie waited for the water to boil and added the pasta. She set the kitchen timer for twelve minutes. Then she wandered into the living room.

"Topeka," Michelle said into the phone. "Topeka is definitely the capital of Kansas."

Stephanie waited for Michelle to hang up. The minutes ticked by. Stephanie glanced impatiently at her watch. She couldn't believe how long Michelle had been talking!

"No, Fargo is in North Dakota, I think," Michelle said.

"Michelle!" Stephanie exploded. "You're hogging the phone forever! Allie tried to call me last night and she couldn't get through. Because you were hogging the phone then too!"

"So?" Michelle asked.

"So, you made me miss a really important call!" Stephanie complained. "The telephone wasn't made so you could do geography homework with your friends."

Michelle put her hand over the receiver. "My calls are important too," she said.

"Well, you have to take turns. Now, hang up." Stephanie reached for the receiver.

"Dad! Dad!" Michelle yelled.

Danny hurried into the living room. "What?" he cried. "What happened?"

"Stephanie won't let me use the phone," Michelle said.

"That's not true, Dad!" Stephanie exclaimed. "Michelle has been on the phone since I got home. What if someone is trying to call me?"

"Well, you do have a point," Danny said. "Someone could be trying to call any of us." He turned to Michelle. "Michelle, honey, sounds like it's time to get off the phone."

Michelle hung up. "This isn't fair, Stephanie," she said.

"Yes, it is," Stephanie insisted.

"No, it's not," Michelle replied.

Brriiing! The kitchen timer went off.

"Dinner's ready," Danny said. "Come in the kitchen. We'll discuss this some more."

Stephanie and Michelle followed Danny into the kitchen.

"If I had my own phone, I wouldn't have this problem," Stephanie mumbled.

"Talking to yourself again, Steph?" Joey teased as Stephanie helped set the table.

"I have to," Stephanie replied. "I don't get to talk to anyone on the *phone*." She glared at Michelle.

"Poor Stephanie," D.J. said. "Hey, why don't I call Becky and Jesse to dinner?" She hurried out to the living room. Stephanie heard her calling up the stairs.

Stephanie stared after her big sister. "Dad, how long will D.J. be gone on her trip?" she asked.

"Ten days," Danny replied. "Why?"

Stephanie's mind was racing. *D.J.'s room will be empty for ten whole days,* she thought.

Actually, the room wasn't empty. It had tons of cool clothes and jewelry in it. Not to mention D.J.'s new CD player. But the most important thing was the phone. A phone with its very own private line.

Stephanie smiled. *I could use the phone whenever I wanted! I'd never miss a call again!*

Plus, she could have totally private conversations with Darcy and Allie!

No more whispering. No more speaking in codes. No more climbing into the closet for privacy. It was too good to be true!

"Dad, I know how to solve the phone problem," Stephanie said. "I could stay in D.J.'s room while she's away!"

"You already have a room of your own," Michelle pointed out.

"I don't have my *own* room," Stephanie said. "I *share* a room—with you. And there is no phone in our room. But there is a phone in D.J.'s room. A

34

very private telephone that no one will be using while she's gone."

"Why should you get the phone?" Michelle asked.

"Because I'm the next oldest. It makes perfect sense," Stephanie answered. She turned a bright smile on her father. "I have really important calls to make, Dad."

"But I have important calls to make too," Michelle cried.

Stephanie scoffed. "You don't even know what important means! Remember the time you dialed nine-one-one to report that Comet swallowed your crayon?"

"That was when I was six and a half," Michelle replied. "And the crayon was periwinkle blue, my favorite color."

Stephanie rolled her eyes. "Come on, Michelle. I should be the one to stay in D.J.'s room."

"No, I should," Michelle insisted.

"No, I should," Stephanie argued.

"Truce!" Danny shouted. He turned to Stephanie. "You do use up your share of phone time, Steph—no one would argue with that."

"Yeah, you don't need your own phone—you need your own switchboard!" Joey joked.

"Well, then, you *both* admit it. I need my own

phone," Stephanie began. "So, naturally, I should—"

Danny held up his hands for silence. "Wait, Stephanie. There's only one fair thing to do," he said. "I'll let you girls decide who deserves to stay in D.J.'s room. You figure out which calls are really important. That way, you'll know who needs D.J.'s phone the most."

Stephanie stared at her father in shock. "You can't be serious! I'm competing with a nine-year-old?"

"Fair is fair," Danny insisted.

Michelle crossed her arms over her chest. "You heard him, Stephanie," she said. "Fair is fair!"

"And now it's fair that everyone helps dish out the food," Danny said. "Because it's time to eat."

As soon as dinner was over. Stephanie rushed to the phone in the living room. She quickly dialed Allie's number. Allie answered right away.

"Hang on a sec," Allie told her. "I'll get Darcy on the other line." She made the three-way phone call.

Once Darcy had answered, Stephanie got right to the point.

"So, what did you decide?" she asked Allie. "You're staying in the Girls Tennis Club, right?"

"She must be. Wasn't it a blast?" Darcy asked.

"The best! And it'll only get better," Stephanie added.

"Your game will improve so much, Allie," Darcy said.

"In fact, I think we need some extra practice right away," Stephanie went on. "Maybe we should—"

"Wait a minute!" Allie cried. "I never even answered your question, Stephanie!"

"What question?" Stephanie asked.

"What I decided about the tennis club," Allie said.

"Well, what are you waiting for?" Darcy asked.

"I was waiting for a chance to get a word in," Allie answered. "And my answer is no. I'm not going to join the club. I'm sorry, guys. But I really want to take guitar lessons. Tennis just isn't my thing."

For a moment, neither Darcy nor Stephanie said anything.

"Hey, you guys, lighten up! We can still play together sometimes, right?" Allie asked.

"I guess so," Darcy admitted. "And I guess if you really want to take guitar lessons, that's cool."

"Don't feel bad," Allie said. "It makes more sense for the two of you to join. I mean, now you guys can be a team. And you won't have to worry about me feeling left out."

"I hadn't thought of that!" Darcy exclaimed.

"Well, I still wish you'd join, Allie," Stephanie said. "But you're right about Darcy and me being partners. Now we won't have to be partners with Sara Albright again."

"Well, I hope we play with Sara again," Darcy put in. "She's so good, she can really help our games."

Playing with Sara feels more like work than like a game, Stephanie thought.

"Couldn't we improve our game without Sara?" Stephanie asked.

"I guess so," Darcy replied. "Hey, why don't we get some extra practice in tomorrow? We can go to my parents' club. Want to?"

"Sounds good to me," Stephanie said.

"Not to me," Allie told them. "Do you mind if I don't come along?"

"I guess not. Okay, then, it'll be just Darcy and me," Stephanie replied.

"Great! Then I'm going to bed early tonight," Darcy said. "That way I'll have extra energy—to play extra hard tomorrow."

"Then I'd better go to bed too," Stephanie said. "Because tomorrow, you, Darcy Powell, are going to see just how great a tennis player I really am!"

CHAPTER
5

◆ ◀ ▪ ◆

"Bye, Mrs. Powell! Thanks for the ride!" Stephanie climbed out of the car and slammed the door.

"Bye, Mom. See you later," Darcy added.

Darcy's mom waved and drove off.

"Wow, this will be fun," Stephanie said. She gazed around in pleasure.

The Marina Sports Club was on the San Francisco waterfront. It was next to a huge green park. Boats were anchored in the water nearby. They bobbed up and down. The sky was clear and a gentle breeze was blowing.

"This is such a cool place to play tennis!" Stephanie cried. "You should come here more often."

"Maybe I will, now that I know someone else who belongs," Darcy replied.

"Someone else?" Stephanie was confused. "Who?"

"Well, Sara, of course," Darcy told her.

Stephanie gazed at Darcy in surprise. "Sara Albright? Darcy, what are you talking about?"

"Don't you remember?" Darcy asked. "Yesterday, at tennis club, I told her my family were members here. She said she wanted to know more about it."

"Yeah, I guess I remember that," Stephanie said. "But how did she become a member already?"

"Well, she's not exactly a member yet. But she will be. I told her all about this place last night," Darcy explained. "So her mother came and checked it out this morning. She agreed that it was great. They're definitely going to join."

"Hold on, hold on," Stephanie cried. "I don't understand. You talked to Sara last night?"

"Sure. After I talked to you," Darcy replied. "I tried to call you back again, Steph, but the line was busy."

"Oh, no! That Michelle . . ." Stephanie moaned. She explained to Darcy about the phone war at home.

"You really could use your own phone," Darcy told her.

"Really!" Stephanie changed the subject. "But

40

why didn't you tell me about Sara in school today?"

"I didn't know everything myself—not until last period," Darcy explained. "That's when Sara told me about joining this club. Right before I invited her."

"Invited her where?" Stephanie asked. Now she was totally confused.

"Here. To play with us today," Darcy replied.

"You invited her to come today?" Stephanie's voice rose. "Why didn't you tell me *that?*"

Darcy shrugged. "I don't know. I didn't think you'd mind. Sara knows so much about tennis! And it's a real challenge to play with her."

"I was kind of looking forward to just the two of us playing today," Stephanie complained.

Darcy glanced at her watch. "Well, it's too late now. Sara should be here soon. She had to go home and get her racket first." Darcy paused. "It *is* okay with you. Isn't it?"

Stephanie hesitated. "Yeah, I guess so."

"Good. Then let's go to my mother's locker," Darcy said. "I need to grab her racket before we start playing."

"What happened to your new racket?" Stephanie asked. "The one with the great sweet spot."

"Oh, Sara said that racket is too light for me. So

I'm going to try my mom's today." Darcy smiled. "Sara knows everything about tennis."

Stephanie didn't say anything. She felt uncomfortable that Darcy had invited Sara. *But she's right,* Stephanie told herself. *Sara does know a lot about tennis.*

Stephanie followed Darcy to the ladies' locker room. Darcy quickly found her mother's racket.

"Here it is!" Darcy announced. "All set."

Stephanie glanced through the windows onto the outdoor court area. There were six tennis courts. And most of them were being used. "Yikes," she said. "There's only one court open. Let's hurry!"

They ran onto the court and began to warm up. Soon she and Darcy had a good rally going.

It was fun to play one-on-one, Stephanie thought. Especially with Darcy. She was slightly better than Stephanie, but she didn't hit the ball too hard or fast, like Sara did.

"Hey, we're getting good at this!" Stephanie called.

"Yeah, what a rally!" Darcy sent the ball sailing back to Stephanie.

"Darcy, your grip is too high on the racket," called a voice from courtside.

"Sara!" Darcy cried. She whirled around. Stephanie's return bounced on the ground behind her.

"Oh! I love your tennis dress," Darcy cried. She jogged across the court to Sara's side.

Sara smiled. "Oh, this is my lucky dress. I won two tournaments in it."

Sara's dress was white with thin purple and blue stripes going up the sides. The stripes perfectly matched the stripes on her socks.

She always looks like a total pro, Stephanie thought. She glanced down at her T-shirt and cutoffs. *Well, at least I'm wearing real tennis shoes today.*

"Hi, Sara," Stephanie called.

"Hi!" Sara answered.

"Whose side do you want to be on?" Darcy asked Sara.

"Why don't I play against both of you? Since I'm a better player," Sara said. She unzipped her racket cover.

"Sure!" Darcy agreed before Stephanie could say anything.

They took their positions on the court with Stephanie and Darcy against Sara.

Sara served and Darcy returned the ball. Sara whacked the ball back—hard—and Darcy raced to hit it back. Then Sara hit it again, then Darcy, then Sara . . .

Am I on this court or not? Stephanie asked herself. *This is not my idea of a good time.*

The next time Sara whacked the ball, Stephanie ran toward it as fast as she could. She reached the ball first.

Finally! she thought. She drew back her racket and hit hard. And sent the ball sailing into the net!

"Whoops!" She groaned. "Sorry, guys."

"Nice try, Stephanie," Sara told her. "But don't choke your grip. And bend your knees more."

Stephanie felt her face turn bright red. *How embarrassing!* Sara made her feel as if she couldn't do anything right.

Then it was Stephanie's turn to serve. As she rallied the ball, she did what Sara said. And returned the ball much more cleanly.

Hmmmm. I guess Sara's comments helped, she thought.

"My serve," Sara called. She sent the ball whizzing toward Stephanie's side of the court.

"Mine!" Darcy shouted.

"Mine!" Stephanie shouted at the same time. She and Darcy both rushed for the ball.

Stephanie drew back her racket, swung—and hit Darcy's racket! The ball fell to the court with a plop.

"Oops!" Stephanie said.

"Stephanie!" Darcy cried out. "I called that ball. Pay more attention."

Boy, she sure is getting serious, Stephanie thought.

"Concentrate, guys," Sara yelled. "Concentration is very important in this game."

"We're sorry, Sara," Darcy called back. She shot a warning look at Stephanie.

"She's right," Darcy said. "We really shouldn't be fooling around out here."

"I'll try harder, promise," Stephanie said.

"Okay." Darcy smiled.

"This one is for you, Stephanie," Sara called.

"Got it!" Stephanie returned the ball, and for a while she and Sara kept up a rally.

"Nice spin on that ball," Sara shouted.

"Thanks!" Stephanie grinned. It was nice to get a compliment from Sara. They continued playing until they had finished a set. Stephanie ran faster and tried harder than she ever had before. *I never knew tennis could be this much work*, she thought. She was out of breath from all the running.

"Hold it," Sara called. She jogged over to Stephanie's side of the court. "I'm dying of thirst," she said. "Can we get something to drink around here?"

"Sure. There's a great snack bar," Darcy said.

"Just water for me," Sara told her. She dug into her pocket for some change.

"We can't all go, can we?" Stephanie asked. "Won't someone else take our court if we leave?"

"You're right," Darcy said. "Two of us should keep playing."

Sara cleared her throat. "Uh, Stephanie, would you mind going? I'd love to try playing singles with Darcy for a while." She gave Stephanie a big smile.

Darcy turned to Stephanie. "Would you, Steph? Sara's such a great player. I'd love to practice one-on-one with her. Just for a bit."

"Oh. Well, okay," Stephanie said with a shrug. "I guess I could go to the snack bar."

"Thanks," Sara said. She handed Stephanie her money. "Cold water for me."

"For me too. Definitely!" Darcy said. "I know I'll work up a thirst playing with Sara!"

Darcy told Stephanie how to get to the snack bar.

"Thanks, Stephanie," Sara said as Stephanie turned to go. "It will be fun to play with someone near my own level."

Stephanie felt her cheeks flame. She stared at the other girl. Sara was smiling, a friendly expression on her face.

She doesn't even know she just insulted me, Stephanie realized.

"I'll be right back," she told Sara and Darcy.

She hurried toward the snack bar. The line was longer than she realized. It took forever to get waited on. Finally it was her turn. She asked for three bottles of water, paid for them, and hurried back to the tennis courts.

Sara and Darcy were in the middle of a rally. They were both frowning in concentration. Both of them had worked up a sweat.

Stephanie sat on the grass at the side of the court. She pulled out her water bottle and took a long drink as she watched them play.

She had to admit that playing with Sara was making Darcy work harder. Darcy was right—Sara could definitely improve her game.

Stephanie glanced at her watch. It was getting late, but neither Sara nor Darcy seemed ready to stop. Finally Darcy missed one of Sara's line drives.

"You forgot to return to center court," Sara called to her. "You should have gotten ready for the next ball, Darcy. That's rule number one."

Stephanie couldn't believe the way Sara pointed out other people's errors. But Darcy bopped herself on the head with her racket and laughed. "You're right, Sara! It won't happen again."

They rallied for a while. Then Darcy missed another ball. It rolled toward Stephanie. "Steph, toss it here!" Darcy called.

Stephanie got up and threw the ball to Darcy. "Darce, it's getting dark out," she said. "How long do we have this court for?"

"Oh!" Darcy cried. She checked her watch. "I didn't realize it was so late!"

"Well, it is," Stephanie said. "Your mom will be here soon to take us home."

"Oh, Stephanie, you never got a chance to play again!" Darcy replied. "I guess I got carried away. Sorry."

"That's okay," Stephanie told her. What else could she say? That she was jealous and feeling left out? *Stop acting like a little kid*, Stephanie told herself.

Still, as Darcy and Sara walked over to her, Stephanie did feel left out. She stooped to pick up their water bottles and handed one to each of them.

"Thanks! I needed this," Sara said. She took a deep swallow. "Though I could keep playing all night," she added. She turned to Darcy.

"You could be a great singles player," Sara told her. "With a little more work you could be up to my speed."

"Really? Wow! Thanks, Sara," Darcy said. Her eyes shone with pleasure at the compliment.

"Well, I'd like to improve my game too, and—" Stephanie began to say.

"Sure. You could learn a lot," Sara told her. She turned to Darcy again.

"You know, Darcy, I just had a great idea." Sara put a hand on Darcy's arm. "You and I could be a team in the Girls Tennis Club!"

What? Stephanie stared at Sara in shock. *Sara and Darcy—a doubles team?*

"I mean, we still have to work on our doubles strategy," Sara said. "But you have tons of talent. What do you think? Wouldn't it be fun?"

'Fun? It would be fantastic, Sara," she said. "We could—" Darcy suddenly stopped in midsentence. She glanced at Stephanie.

Stephanie stood there, frozen to the spot. She didn't know what to do or say. She wanted to scream out, *Don't do it, Darcy! Don't leave me out!* Talk about acting like a baby. Instead, she bit her tongue and kept quiet.

Darcy licked her lips. "Well, I mean, it would be fun," she told Sara, "but ..."

"But what?" Sara asked. "What's the problem?"

"Well, Stephanie and I thought we would be partners," Darcy said. "But the two of us could play with you too."

"Oh," Sara said. She glanced at Stephanie. "Okay, sure."

Stephanie let out a big whoosh of air. She realized that she had been holding her breath, waiting for Darcy's answer. But now that she'd heard it, she was totally relieved.

Did Sara really think that Darcy would team up with her? And dump Stephanie?

No way, Sara, Stephanie thought. *Darcy's my best friend. She would never dump me like that. Never!*

CHAPTER
6

◆ ◀ ▪ ◆

"Let's get moving, Stephanie!" Ms. Spano's voice echoed through the empty girls' locker room. "Everyone's already out on the courts."

"I'm sorry, Ms. Spano," Stephanie said breathlessly. She quickly changed into her shorts for the tennis club meeting.

Darcy's going to kill me for being late, Stephanie thought as she pulled her hair back. *She's so totally pumped up about tennis. She didn't talk about anything else all week.*

"You need to sign up with a doubles partner today," Ms. Spano said. "Everyone's signed up except Gwenith. So add your name to the list."

Ms. Spano handed her a clipboard. Stephanie

grabbed the pencil attached by a string. She scanned the list.

"Darcy probably signed us up as partners already," Stephanie said. "Here it is. Darcy Powell and—" Stephanie gasped. "No way!" she exclaimed.

"What's wrong?" Ms. Spano asked.

"This says Darcy Powell and Sara Albright!" Stephanie glanced up at the teacher. "It must be a mistake. Maybe Sara signed them up. Because Darcy is *my* partner."

Ms. Spano frowned. "No, I'm pretty sure Darcy signed this list herself."

Stephanie looked back down at the list. She felt her stomach drop. Ms. Spano was right. It was definitely Darcy's handwriting. She recognized her best friend's loopy signature—the same signature that Darcy put on every note she had ever left for Stephanie.

Darcy had signed herself up with Sara!

"Hurry up and change," Ms. Spano told her. "We'll clear this up outside."

You bet we'll clear this up! Stephanie thought. *Because there must be some explanation. Maybe it's even a weird joke!*

It had to be a joke, Stephanie thought. She sat down and began to lace up her tennis shoes. But her fingers felt as if they were made out of lead.

She had to try three times before her sneakers were finally tied tight.

Then she jumped up and raced for the door. She absolutely had to find Darcy. She had to know what was going on. She threw open the door—and found herself face-to-face with Gwenith.

The short girl jumped in surprise. "Oh, Stephanie!" she said. "Ms. Spano said I should come get you. But I guess you're already on your way!"

"I've got to hurry, Gwenith," Stephanie said, pushing past her. "I have to find Darcy."

"Darcy's on the courts already," Gwenith said. She had to run to keep up with Stephanie. "She's rallying with Sara. They got here early."

"That must have been Sara's idea," Stephanie muttered.

She spotted Darcy and Sara playing singles and started toward them.

"Uh, Stephanie, our court is this way." Gwenith pointed in the opposite direction.

"But I need to talk to Darcy first," Stephanie said.

Gwenith seemed embarrassed. "Oh. I was afraid you wouldn't want to be partners with me," she said.

Stephanie felt herself flush. "It's not that. I just have to see Darcy."

"Well, I'll wait for you, okay?" Gwenith asked.

"Sure, okay." Stephanie hurried over to Darcy and Sara's court.

"Darcy, can I talk to you?" Stephanie called.

Darcy glanced over at Sara. Then she walked over to Stephanie. "Hi, Steph!" She gave Stephanie an extra-bright smile.

"Darcy, what's going on?" Stephanie demanded. "Did you really sign up to be Sara's partner?"

"Well, you see, I . . ." Darcy started to say.

Before she could finish, Sara rushed up to them. "Hey, Stephanie," she called. "Ready for some intense doubles practice? Ms. Spano promised we'd really get serious today. So I snagged Darcy as my partner. You know she's the only one here who's good enough to play doubles with me."

"Yeah. Well, maybe, but . . ." Stephanie stammered.

"I knew you wouldn't mind," Sara said. "So maybe we'll all get together again sometime and fool around? Come on, Darcy." Sara grabbed Darcy's arm. "Ms. Spano said not to waste time. Bye, Stephanie!" Sara gave a little wave.

Stephanie stood there with her mouth open. *I can't believe it! Sara didn't give Darcy a chance to say anything!*

"Steph—can we warm up?" Gwenith called.

Stephanie turned. She sighed. Darcy was definitely going to play with Sara, and she was stuck with Gwenith.

She hurried over to Gwenith. She glanced at her hopeful smile and smiled back. "Yeah, let's go," she said.

She and Gwenith began to warm up. But Stephanie couldn't help glancing over at Darcy's court from time to time. Sara had an amazingly strong backhand. And that killer serve. Lots of other kids on the team were watching Sara too, Stephanie noticed. Even Ms. Spano stopped to compliment her.

"Wow, Sara's really something!" Gwenith said. "I hope I never have to play against her."

"Well, I'm sure you'll get better fast," Stephanie said.

"Think so?" Gwenith seemed doubtful. "I mean, I really like tennis, but I'm not nearly as good as you are, Stephanie."

"Thanks," Stephanie told her. *But obviously Sara thinks that I'm nowhere near as good as Darcy.*

"Let's take a few minutes to practice serves, people!" Ms. Spano called. "Everyone watch Sara—she has nearly perfect form!"

Sara served a half dozen balls over the net while Ms. Spano pointed out everything that she did right.

"Now everyone try to match Sara's form," Ms. Spano instructed.

"You go first," Gwenith told Stephanie. "I'll never be able to do it."

"Well, okay." Stephanie threw the ball up and drew back her racket the way Sara had. She swung with all her might. To her horror, the racket flew into the air!

She gave a shriek as it crashed back down. Stephanie stared at it in disbelief. There was a moment of silence. Then Gwenith burst out laughing.

Stephanie felt the blood rush to her cheeks. She snatched up the racket and glanced over at Sara and Darcy's court.

Please don't let them laugh, she thought. To her relief, she realized that Darcy and Sara were busy demonstrating serves to some other players.

Stephanie let herself grin. "Guess I better practice some more," she called out to Gwenith.

Gwenith grinned back. *She's not so bad to play with*, Stephanie found herself thinking.

When they were done with the drill, Ms. Spano put them in teams to practice playing doubles. Stephanie and Gwenith were on one team, playing against Maggie Shapiro and Kira Weston. Maggie and Kira were fairly good players, about on Stephanie's level.

"Yours!" Stephanie called.

Gwenith ran toward the ball as fast as she could—which wasn't very fast. No way could she ever hit it back! Stephanie ran up quickly and swatted the ball over the net.

"Sorry!" Gwenith called. "Thanks," she said breathlessly.

"No problem," Stephanie replied. "You know, Gwenith, you're not a bad player. You can return the ball okay—when you get there in time."

"I know—I'm so slow!" Gwenith moaned.

"You just need to get in better shape," Stephanie told her. Just then Stephanie heard Darcy scream out, "Yes! We did it, Sara! We won!"

Stephanie looked over to see Darcy jump into the air and high-five Sara. Sara beamed at her. "You're really improving," she told Darcy. Darcy gazed at Sara as if she were her hero. Stephanie frowned.

"Okay, everybody, let's wrap it up!" Ms. Spano called. "See you next week."

Everyone headed for the locker rooms.

"Maybe you're right about my getting in shape," Gwenith said. She was breathing heavily as they walked along.

"Right," Stephanie replied. She wasn't really listening. She was watching Sara and Darcy. Their heads were close together as they talked. She could hear Darcy laughing at something Sara had said.

I can't believe this, Stephanie thought. *Darcy acts like she's forgotten all about me!*

"I mean, I knew I was out of shape," Gwenith went on, "but I didn't know it was *this* bad! Stephanie, you're not even breathing hard. How do you do it?"

"Huh? Oh, you know. I go rollerblading, and biking and stuff." Stephanie opened the door to the locker room.

I have to talk to Darcy alone, away from Sara, she thought. *And that's not going to be easy.*

Stephanie changed quickly. She slung her backpack over her shoulder and searched for Darcy. Finally, she spotted her heading for the locker room door.

"Darce!" Stephanie called. "Wait up!"

Darcy turned. "Oh, gee, Steph, I have to go!" she said. "My mom is waiting for me out front. I, uh, I have a dentist appointment."

"But we have to talk, and—" Stephanie began.

"Really, Stephanie, I have to go. I'll call you!" Darcy waved and ran out the door.

Stephanie stared after her.

Am I wrong, she wondered, *or is my best friend acting like she's* not *my best friend anymore?*

CHAPTER
7

◆ ◀ ▶ ◆

Stephanie burst through the front door and ran for the phone. It had taken forever to get home. Gwenith had walked with her—slowly. Gwenith was still winded from the tennis match. It had taken forever.

As soon as Gwenith turned off at her corner, Stephanie had sprinted the rest of the way home. She needed to call Allie and tell her about Darcy and Sara. She needed advice—and fast.

Stephanie stopped short in front of the telephone. "Oh, no! Not again!" she cried.

Michelle was on the phone. She sat sideways in her chair with one leg slung over the side. Her finger was twisted up in the phone cord. She looked as if she planned to talk forever.

"Well, my friend Amy named hers Wendy," Michelle said into the receiver. "And Megan named hers Toby."

Stephanie sighed. But she decided to give Michelle five minutes before complaining to her father. *After all*, she reminded herself, *fair is fair.*

Stephanie headed into the kitchen. Danny, D.J., and Joey were making a huge pile of sandwiches.

"Hi, Steph," Danny said. "You're just in time for dinner. It's just us tonight—Jesse, Becky, and the twins are out at a birthday party."

"Yeah. We're having sandwiches," D.J. added.

"My famous peanut butter and banana sandwiches," Joey told her. "And they'll be ready any minute."

"Mmm, peanut butter and banana. Just what I need after working up a thirst at tennis," Stephanie teased. She poured herself a glass of lemonade and gulped it down.

She poked her head back into the living room to check on Michelle.

"Well, Cassie, I'm not sure," Michelle was saying. "I could change her name to Penny. What do you think?"

Stephanie turned to her dad. "Dad, how long has Michelle been on the phone?" she asked.

"I'm not sure, Steph. I wasn't timing her," Danny said.

"At least as long as this peanut butter has been stuck to the roof of my mouth," Joey said through a mouthful of food.

Stephanie felt anger bubbling up inside her. She stormed into the living room toward Michelle.

"Hi, Mandy," Michelle said.

"Mandy?" Stephanie cried. "Now you're talking to Mandy? Get off the phone, Michelle! I really need it!"

"But this is a very important call," Michelle told her. "And Dad said whoever had an important call got to use the phone first."

Michelle spoke into the receiver again. "Why don't you name him Cinnamon?" she asked. "Gerbils might not come when they're called, Mandy. But you've got to name them something."

"That's it!" Stephanie shouted. She rushed back into the kitchen. "Dad, you've got to get Michelle off the phone! She's talking about gerbils! Gerbils! I need to make a really important call, and she's naming pets!"

Danny went to the living room door. "Michelle, honey, you have to get off now," he called. "Stephanie needs to use the phone, too."

Michelle slammed down the phone and ran into

the kitchen. "But I wasn't done yet," she protested. "Why does Stephanie get the phone?"

"Because!" Stephanie said. "Dad, we have got to have some rules around here! We have a rule about showers—three minutes each. We should limit phone calls too!"

"I know, Steph, you're absolutely right," Danny said. "With nine people in this house, we do need better phone rules."

Joey looked thoughtful. "We used to have a ten-minute rule," he said."

"But Michelle broke it," D.J. pointed out. "Because she started talking on the phone before she knew how to tell time."

"I think we had a twenty-minute rule once," Joey said.

"But D.J. broke that when she got her first boyfriend," Danny remarked.

D.J. smiled dreamily. "I remember that," she said.

"Well, a time limit is still a good idea," Danny said. "As soon as Becky and Jesse get home, we'll have a family meeting. Will that be okay, Steph?"

"That would be great!" Stephanie replied. "And in the meantime, it's *my* turn to make a call."

Stephanie headed for the phone in the living

room. She dialed Allie's number. Allie answered right away.

"Allie! You'll never believe what happened at tennis today," Stephanie said. She poured out the whole story. "Darcy played with Sara the whole time. And she wouldn't even talk to me about it," Stephanie finished.

"Well, maybe Sara made her sign up," Allie said.

"I *know* it was Sara's idea," Stephanie told her. "She already asked Darcy to be her partner. It happened the other day at the tennis club. And right in front of me too!"

"So, why didn't Darcy say no?" Allie asked.

"She did! That's why I'm so upset," Stephanie explained. "Because when I got to tennis club today, Darcy had signed up as Sara's partner anyway."

"Maybe Ms. Spano paired them up," Allie suggested.

"No," Stephanie insisted. "It was Darcy's handwriting. And Ms. Spano said Darcy decided." Stephanie felt tears welling up in her eyes. She took a deep breath. "Oh, Allie. What am I going to do?"

"Be calm, Stephanie. Darcy's still your friend," Allie said. "This is only tennis club. Anyway, maybe you and Darcy will play together at the next club meeting."

"Not if Sara has her way, we won't," Stephanie replied. "Besides, now I'm stuck with Gwenith. I mean, Gwenith is really nice, but she's the worst player in the whole club. I had to save almost every ball that went to her—and we still lost our game!"

"How did Sara and Darcy do?" Allie asked.

"They won, naturally. They're the best players in the club," Stephanie said. "Tons better than Gwenith and me, that's for sure. Once, Gwenith even hit the ball into the wrong court!"

"You're kidding!" Allie cracked up.

"Sara laughed too. She's such a snob!" Stephanie complained. "I don't know why Darcy wants to play with her at all."

"Maybe she's just being nice. Sara is new in school," Allie replied.

"Well, if Sara wants to make friends, she can start by not stealing my friend away from me," Stephanie said.

"She could never do that," Allie assured her. "You, me, and Darcy are best friends."

"That's what I used to think," Stephanie told her. "But it sure didn't feel that way today. Not when Darcy wouldn't even talk to me. She said she had to go to the dentist, and ran off."

Allie was silent for a moment. "I know!" she suddenly said. "Let's go to the mall tomorrow. You, me, and Darcy. We'll catch a movie or something."

"Maybe she won't come," Stephanie said.

"I'll call her," Allie offered. "And don't worry. Nothing could come between the three of us. We're best friends—forever!"

Stephanie could barely wait for Becky, Jesse, and the twins to come home. Finally, they walked in the front door.

"Hi, everybody!" Becky called.

"Great! Now we can take our vote!" Stephanie led everyone into the kitchen. "House meeting!" she yelled.

They all took a seat around the table. Danny explained that they were going to decide on a time limit for phone calls.

"Why don't we go around in a circle?" Danny suggested. "Each person votes on how many minutes we should be allowed to talk."

"I think fifteen minutes is fair," Becky said.

"Sometimes that isn't long enough," D.J. said. "So I vote for thirty minutes."

"Thirty minutes is a long time for the phone to be busy," Stephanie pointed out. "So maybe it should be fifteen minutes. But if it's really important, you can call back for *another* fifteen minutes."

"I agree to that," Joey said.

"I don't," Michelle said. "Because Stephanie always says my calls aren't important. And they are!"

"Not always, Michelle," Stephanie told her.

"Always," Michelle insisted. "And that's why I should get to use the phone in D.J.'s room and—"

"Not fair!" Stephanie shouted. "We're not talking about that now, Dad, and—"

"Hold on!" Danny held up his hands for quiet. "I told you girls to decide about D.J.'s phone yourselves. So, how many minutes do you vote for, Michelle?"

"Well, twenty-five minutes," Michelle answered.

"And I say twenty minutes, with no call-back," Jesse said.

Nicky raised his hand. "I want to vote too," he announced.

"Me too," Alex said.

Danny sighed. "Okay, give us your votes," he said.

The twins both said four—because that's how old they were.

"Okay. And I vote for twelve minutes," Danny announced. "Now I'll add up all the times and get an average. That way everybody will be happy." He took a calculator out of a kitchen drawer and started pressing buttons. "I get an average of sixteen minutes," he said.

"How will I know when my time is up?" Michelle asked. "I don't have a watch."

"Well, you could get the egg timer in the kitchen," Danny suggested.

"Right! Just don't boil your eggs as long as you talk on the phone," Joey joked. "Or else you'll have an egg-stremely overcooked egg. Or it might even egg-splode!"

Michelle laughed. "That's funny, Joey. But set the timer now, because it's my turn to use the phone again."

Before Stephanie could say anything, Michelle raced into the living room. She was on the phone again!

Well, at least I know that I have to wait only sixteen minutes, Stephanie thought, glancing at her watch.

The sixteen minutes crept slowly by. It seemed like an awfully long time. Stephanie was fuming. She just *had* to talk to Darcy! Allie was probably trying to do a three-way call this very second. She went into the living room.

"No, Audrey," Michelle said. "Wednesday is tacos, Thursday is pizza, and Friday is . . ."

Stephanie moaned. Michelle was discussing the lunch menu!

I can't stand it, Stephanie thought. *I have to get in touch with Allie right now!*

Stephanie took the stairs two at a time. She rushed into her dad's study and picked up the extension phone. "Michelle? Audrey? Listen, guys, this is really an emergency. I need to talk on the phone for two minutes, that's all."

A recorded voice said, "Please dial again or hang up."

What? Stephanie stared at the phone. Then she hung up and raced back downstairs. Michelle still sat in the chair, talking. The egg timer was still ticking away.

"Michelle!" Stephanie shouted. "I just heard a recording on the line! Are you talking to Audrey or not?"

"Uh, well . . ." Michelle said.

Stephanie grabbed the phone out of her sister's hand. She listened closely. *Please hang up and dial again,* she heard.

"Michelle, who are you talking to?" Stephanie demanded.

"Nobody," Michelle admitted. "I was pre-

68

tending to talk to Audrey. But I was only going to pretend for sixteen minutes."

"I can't believe this!" Stephanie wailed. "How could you do this to me? I've been dying to get hold of Allie!"

Michelle crossed her arms. "But I want to stay in D.J.'s room and use her phone," she said. "So I had to prove that I make important phone calls too."

"Fine!" Stephanie snapped. "I give up! Stay in D.J.'s room! Use her phone. At least it will keep you from tying up *this* phone all night."

Michelle's eyes lit up. "Really?" she cried.

"Yes," Stephanie said. "Tomorrow you get D.J.'s phone. I never want to wait for you to finish a pretend call again!"

Stephanie stomped up the stairs to her room. She shut the door with a bang. She flung herself on her bed and stared at the ceiling.

I can't believe I just did that, she thought. I just gave away a chance for my own private telephone for a week!

"Oh, well," she murmured. "What do I need my own phone for anyway? My best friend doesn't even want to talk to me!"

CHAPTER
8

◆ ◀ ◆ ◆

"Did you pack extra socks, D.J.?" Danny asked. "You should always have warm, dry socks when you're near the water."

"Dad, if I pack one more thing, my suitcase will explode!" D.J. answered.

It was Saturday morning, and D.J. was about to leave on her field trip. She sat on her overstuffed suitcase while Becky tried to lock it. The entire family had gathered in her room to see her off.

Stephanie rubbed the sleep from her eyes and yawned. "Maybe I should sit on the suitcase with Becky," Stephanie said.

"No, thanks," D.J. said. "I don't want to break it—just close it."

"Did you remember to roll everything instead of

folding it when you packed?" Danny asked. "Maybe that's why your suitcase won't close."

"I rolled, Dad," D.J. answered. "But I didn't roll my sunblock, and the first aid kit, and all the other extra supplies you made me pack."

Danny looked hurt. "I'm just making sure you have everything you need. You can never be too careful when it comes to packing for trips."

"I don't really think I'll need the inflatable life vest you gave me," D.J. said. "That's the one thing I didn't pack!"

"Would you like to take my extra flashlight?" Joey asked. "It's perfect in an emergency."

"There won't be any emergencies," D.J. said hastily. "But thanks for the offer, Joey."

"That's a relief," Joey joked. "I don't think I could sleep at night without my flashlight under the pillow."

"I don't think I *could* sleep with a flashlight under my pillow," D.J. cracked.

Suddenly Becky yelled. "Got it! The suitcase is closed!" She snapped the locks and D.J. jumped off.

"This is it," D.J. said. Everyone lined up to hug her good-bye.

"Don't worry about your room while you're

gone," Stephanie whispered. "I'll keep an eye on it."

"I heard that!" Michelle cried. "And I won't touch anything in your room, D.J. Not even your box of love letters that's underneath the sweaters on your top shelf."

"Michelle!" D.J. yelled. "Don't you dare snoop through my things!"

"Okay, okay," Michelle said, rolling her eyes. "I won't, I promise."

Danny checked his watch. "Time to go," he said. "Come on, D.J., or we won't be on time to meet the rest of your marine biology class."

Danny picked up D.J.'s suitcase. D.J. grabbed her backpack. She paused at the door to her room. "Well, bye, everyone," she called. "I'll see you all in ten days."

"Isn't Darcy here yet?" Stephanie asked Allie. She plopped onto the bench near the main entrance to the mall. She tried to catch her breath. She had run through the mall to be on time.

She had made it to their usual meeting spot. Allie was already waiting. But Darcy was nowhere in sight.

"She's probably running a little late," Allie said.

"She's running late?" Stephanie asked. "That's

funny, because I just about killed myself to get here in time. D.J. left this morning and there were a million things to do."

"Well, you're here now," Allie said. "And Darcy will be here soon too."

"I know. Actually, I'm a little nervous," she admitted. "What am I going to say to her?" she asked. "So, Darcy, exactly why did you sign up to be Sara's partner?"

"You can't say that," Allie told her. "And anyway, I'm sure she had a good reason."

"I hope so." Stephanie gave Allie a pleading look. "Allie, are you sure you don't want to join the Girls Tennis Club? Are you really absolutely, positively going to stick with guitar lessons? I really, really miss you!"

Allie laughed. "Nice try. But I'm not quitting guitar. I had a private lesson yesterday, and it was really fun." Allie paused. "Anyway, you and Gwenith could get better at tennis," she said.

"I hope so," Stephanie answered. "Still, I wish you and me and Darcy were on the same team. That's the way I thought it would be. The three of us best friends together, like always."

"I know," Allie replied. "But we don't have to do everything together," Allie went on. "I mean, you like writing for the school paper, but Darcy and I don't. And you do it anyway, right?"

"Of course," Stephanie said.

"Well, I like guitar and you don't. But I'm going to do it anyway," Allie said. "We don't have to do the same thing all the time, you know. That doesn't mean we aren't best friends."

"I guess so," Stephanie said with a sigh. "I guess friends don't have to do everything together."

"Right! Like, I'm not at all mad that Darcy slept over Sara's last night without us," Allie continued.

Stephanie's mouth dropped open. "What? Darcy slept over at Sara's?"

Allie flushed. "Oh. Yeah."

"When did you find that out?" Stephanie demanded.

"When I called Darcy last night about coming to the mall. She was just about to leave for Sara's. She probably would have told you if you'd called her last night too," Allie said.

"I couldn't!" Stephanie cried. "Michelle was hogging the phone again."

Allie shook her head. "Don't worry. I think Darcy likes Sara just because she's so into tennis. Darcy's still our friend. You'll see. As soon as she gets here, everything will be fine," Allie added.

"*If* she ever gets here," Stephanie said, glancing at her watch. "She's thirty minutes late."

"She isn't usually this late," Allie admitted.

"Maybe she forgot the plan. After all, she was with Sara this morning," Stephanie pointed out.

Allie frowned. "Maybe she got mixed up and went to meet us at the food court. Let's go look. And if she's not there, we'll call her parents."

"Or Sara's house," Stephanie said. "I bet they went out to play tennis. I bet she really did forget about us."

"Stephanie," Allie said. "You've got to stop. You sound as if you're, like, jealous or something."

"I'm not jealous," Stephanie replied.

"Then what are you?" Allie challenged.

"I don't know what I am, but I am *not* jealous of Sara," Stephanie insisted. "Just because Darcy thinks Sara is so cool, and that she's the greatest tennis player in the world, and just because Darcy doesn't tell me when she's going to hang out with Sara instead of me, that doesn't mean I'm jealous."

"If you say so," Allie replied.

They headed for the food court. On the way they passed the sporting goods store.

"Allie, wait," Stephanie said. "I want to look at tennis skirts. It's getting embarrassing, wearing cutoffs to practice. Maybe I could find something nice on sale."

"We're supposed to be looking for Darcy," Allie reminded her.

"This will only take a second. I won't even try anything on. I'll just see what they have." Stephanie examined the clothes in the window. "Maybe they have the kind of thing some of the girls in the Girls Tennis Club are wearing."

"You mean the kind that Sara wears," Allie said with a half-smile.

"Whatever," Stephanie replied. "Let's just bop in and out, and then we'll go find Darcy."

"Darcy will be mad if we keep her waiting."

Stephanie frowned at her best friend. "Allie, we've been waiting for Darcy for half an hour! She can wait for five minutes while I look at a tennis dress." She marched into the store.

Allie sighed and followed her. "Okay, but be quick," she insisted. "Darcy's probably on her fourth bagel by now."

"I don't think so," Stephanie said. She stopped short, and Allie bumped into her.

"Now what?" Allie asked.

"Well, Darcy is definitely not in the food court, waiting for us," Stephanie said.

She pointed toward the women's clothing section. Darcy stood in front of a full-length mirror, examining her reflection. She wore a pleated green tennis skirt.

The dressing room door opened and Sara walked out.

"Mine doesn't fit," Sara complained. She stood next to Darcy in front of the mirror.

Sara was wearing an identical green skirt. She and Darcy looked like twins!

CHAPTER
9

♦ ◄ ◗ ♦

"I'm leaving," Stephanie said. She spun around. All she could think about was getting out of the store and away from Darcy and Sara.

But Allie grabbed her arm. "Wait, Steph. I'm sure Darcy can explain." Allie turned around. "Darcy! There you are!" she called. "We were waiting for you by the entrance. You were supposed to be there at ten o'clock."

Darcy looked up in surprise. She glanced back and forth between Stephanie and Allie.

"Oh, no!" she cried. "I totally forgot about meeting you guys. I can't believe it!"

Well, I can believe it, Stephanie thought. *Especially since you were with Sara.*

"You guys must think I'm crazy. I'm really

sorry." Darcy rushed up to them, shaking her head. "I was in such a rush last night, and then when we got here today, I saw these skirts on sale, and Sara and I both loved them. I just wasn't thinking about anything else."

Sara stepped up. "Aren't these skirts cute?" Sara asked. "Darcy and I figured that since we're a doubles team now, we should really dress alike."

"Yeah," Darcy said. "Then we'll look like a professional team." Darcy smiled at Sara.

Stephanie couldn't believe what she was hearing. Darcy didn't even seem embarrassed about choosing Sara as her partner! She hadn't even apologized to Stephanie.

Stephanie's heart began to pound. Darcy had never done anything like this to her before.

"I'm going to try a different size," Sara said, holding another skirt up to her waist. "Be right back."

Sara disappeared into the dressing room.

Stephanie took a deep breath. "Darcy, how could you sign up as Sara's partner without even telling me?" she blurted out.

Darcy looked down at the floor. "I guess I should have told you, Steph," she admitted. "I meant to! But then you were late for practice, and we had to sign up right away. I would have explained after practice, but my mother was waiting for me."

"But we joined the club so we could play tennis together," Stephanie told her.

"I know. And we're still in the club, only Sara's my partner now, that's all. You and I can still play together anytime," Darcy said. "But you know that Sara is the best player on the team. I can learn a lot by being her partner. I really didn't think you'd mind."

"But what about today? How could you forget about meeting Allie and me?" Stephanie asked, her voice rising. "Friends aren't supposed to forget about each other. And friends aren't supposed to dump their friends either."

"I didn't dump you," Darcy replied. "I decided to pair up with Sara, that's all. She *is* the best player on the team."

"You already said that," Stephanie pointed out.

The dressing room door burst open with a bang. Sara waltzed out wearing a different size green tennis skirt.

"This one is perfect!" she announced. She pulled Darcy over next to her. "They are so cool," Sara said. "We look like a real doubles team now."

"Uh, Steph, weren't you going to look for a tennis outfit too?" Allie asked.

"Oh, you should, Stephanie," Sara said. "It's important to have the right look on the court. A winning team has to have winning clothes," she added.

Stephanie felt herself flush with anger. "Aren't you getting a little carried away with this winning-team stuff?" she said. "I mean, it's only the middle school tennis club. Not the pros."

"Well, Darcy and I are serious about being a winning team," Sara replied.

"She's right," Darcy told her. "And the only way you're going to win is if you have the right attitude."

"Totally," Sara agreed. "When you're a serious athlete, attitude is everything." She nudged Darcy. "And it doesn't hurt to have killer strategy."

"What's that mean?" Stephanie demanded.

"It means Darcy and I do more than talk about our game," Sara answered. "We're really working as a team. Ms. Spano will never teach you the kind of doubles strategy I already know."

"You guys are acting like you're tennis stars or something," Stephanie cried. "Give me a break! You're not that great."

"Says you," Darcy snapped. "You don't have to insult us, Stephanie. I can't help it if Sara and I happen to be the best players in the club. I'm sorry if you can't handle that."

"What makes you so sure you're the best in the club?" Stephanie shot back.

"Because we are," Darcy said.

"If you think you're so hot, then why don't you prove it?" Stephanie said.

"Uh, Steph . . ." Allie nudged her in the side. Stephanie knew she was losing it, but she couldn't help it. The way Darcy and Sara were acting just made her so mad!

"Prove it?" Darcy repeated.

"Yeah. Prove it!" Stephanie exclaimed. "I challenge you to a tennis match! Gwenith and me against you and Sara."

Darcy laughed. "No way! You and Gwenith could never beat Sara and me, Stephanie! And you know it!"

"You're just afraid to face us on the courts after all your bragging," Stephanie said. "I dare you!"

"Fine!" Darcy snapped. "We accept the challenge."

"Fine!" Stephanie snapped back. "Meet us at the courts at ten o'clock. Next Saturday!" Stephanie spun around and marched out of the store without looking back.

"Stephanie, wait up!" Allie called. "Wait for me."

Stephanie was so mad, she didn't hear Allie at first. Allie finally caught up to her in the mall and grabbed her arm.

"Stephanie, what did you just say? Are you crazy? You can't beat Sara and Darcy!" Allie cried.

Stephanie blinked. She stared at her best friend. "You know something, Allie?" she asked. "You're right!"

Stephanie dropped her head into her hands and groaned. "Oh, Allie, what are we going to do? Darcy and Sara are going to destroy us!"

CHAPTER
10

◆ ◀ ◆ ◆

"Stephanie, we've circled the mall two times now," Allie complained. "I'm going to get dizzy soon if you don't slow down."

"Sorry," Stephanie said. She stopped in her tracks. "Allie, I must have lost my mind! What was I thinking?"

"I don't know, Steph," Allie told her. "But let's go to the food court. I think better on a full stomach."

Stephanie followed Allie across the mall. She glanced at her watch. "We'll have to eat fast. I've got be home in an hour to watch Michelle and the twins."

"That's okay. That's plenty of time to eat," Allie told her.

"Yeah, but we also need to figure out how to fix this mess I made. I think we need a *serious* plan," Stephanie said.

In the food court, Allie bought juice and a bagel. Stephanie paced up and down behind her.

"Come on, let's share this," Allie said. "Steph? Are you going to sit down?"

Stephanie jumped. "Huh? Oh, yeah." She dropped into a chair next to Allie.

"I know I shouldn't have opened my big mouth," Stephanie said. "But Darcy just made me so mad! I can't believe the way she's acting! Like she and Darcy are professional athletes with their matching skirts and everything!"

"They were pretty obnoxious," Allie agreed. "But you should never have challenged them."

"Allie, whose side are you on anyway?" Stephanie asked.

"Why don't you call Darcy later and tell her you're sorry?" Allie suggested. "Or you could say you were just joking and you didn't really mean it."

"Not even!" Stephanie protested. "I can't take back what I said. Then Darcy and Sara will *really* think they're hot stuff. And I'll look like a total jerk. Forget that."

Allie looked hurt.

85

"Sorry, Allie," Stephanie said, softening her voice. "It's just that I don't want to look like a total dweeb. I can't back down. I just need a plan."

"You have only a week until your challenge match," Allie pointed out. "It better be a *great* plan."

"It will be," Stephanie said. She thought for a while. Suddenly, she snapped her fingers.

"I've got it!" she cried. "I know exactly what to do. As soon as I get home, I'll call Gwenith and tell her about the match. Then all we have to do is start some serious training. We can be ready in time. We'll need to work mostly on our strength and endurance."

"Don't forget about your doubles strategy," Allie reminded her.

"Right. That too. But mostly I've got to convince Gwenith that she can be as good a player as Darcy or Sara."

Allie laughed in surprise. "Stephanie, *you're* not even as good as Darcy or Sara! How do you expect Gwenith to believe that?"

Stephanie shrugged. "I haven't figured that one out yet, Allie," she said. "But I'll let you know as soon as I do."

"You *do* need help. Maybe I'd better come with you," Allie said.

Stephanie called home and her aunt Becky came to pick them up at the mall. They drove back to Stephanie's house. Becky pulled up to the curb. She honked the horn and Jesse hurried out.

"Thanks for watching the kids," Becky told Stephanie. "I told them you'd give them lunch."

"No problem," Stephanie said.

Jesse opened the car door. He grinned at Stephanie and Allie. "Have fun with the monsters," he said. "Becky and I will be back in time for dinner."

Becky and Jesse drove off. Stephanie and Allie hurried into the house. Stephanie headed for the phone.

"I'll call Gwenith right away," she said.

"Think again," Allie told her. She pointed into the living room.

Michelle was talking on the telephone.

"Michelle!" Stephanie cried. "Why aren't you using D.J.'s phone?"

Michelle covered the mouthpiece with her hand. "I had to watch Nicky and Alex until you came inside."

Stephanie glanced at her cousins. They were running up and down the living room with a stuffed bear.

Stephanie sighed. "Come on, Allie." She led the

way up to D.J.'s room. She picked up her sister's phone.

"Wait!" Stephanie cried. "How are Gwenith and I going to work on our doubles strategy? We don't have a doubles team to play against!" Stephanie closed her eyes. "This is a nightmare!"

"Maybe I could play against you two," Allie offered.

"There's no way you can give us the kind of competition that Darcy and Sara can." Stephanie sighed. "But you'll have to do."

"Thanks a lot," Allie said. She looked hurt again.

"Oh, I didn't mean it like that," Stephanie told her. "Anyway, even if you play, we still need a second player. Who can we find at such short notice?"

"Maybe Gwenith knows someone," Allie suggested.

"Good idea," Stephanie said. She punched Gwenith's number. Gwenith answered after two rings.

"Hi, Gwenith, it's Stephanie," she said, pretending to be casual. "Uh, are you enjoying your Saturday?"

"Oh, definitely," Gwenith said. "Saturday is my favorite day. Sleep late, watch cartoons all morning, you know how it goes. Weekends are for totally slacking off, right?"

"So you don't have any plans for the afternoon?"

"I was going to read a magazine and listen to a new CD, maybe watch some TV. Why?"

"Well, actually, Gwen—" Stephanie took a deep breath and began talking fast. "It's like this. I sort of challenged Darcy and Sara to a tennis match next Saturday. And I told them that you and I could beat them. Which shouldn't be a problem, as long as we start training now. And then train every day until Saturday. So what do you say, Gwenith? Are you up for it?"

"Darcy and Sara?" Gwenith said. "You told them we could beat them? Stephanie, are you crazy?"

"Gwenith, we can do it," Stephanie said firmly. "I know we can. All we need is the right attitude. You can't win unless you have a winning attitude."

I can't believe I just said that, Stephanie said to herself. *I sound just like Darcy and Sara!*

"So, Gwenith—it's off the couch and onto the courts," she said. "Remember, I have faith in you. We'll just have to work really, really hard, that's all."

There was silence on the other end of the phone.

"Gwenith? Are you still there?" Stephanie asked.

"I'm here, Stephanie. I'm just thinking about all

this. I guess it might be good. I mean, I decided to join the Girls Tennis Club to get in shape."

"Great!" Stephanie said. "That's the spirit, Gwenith! This is the perfect chance to whip yourself into top-notch condition." Stephanie paused. "There's just one problem. We need a fourth player for this afternoon. Allie will play, but she needs a partner. Can you think of anyone who could play today?"

"Ummm, my brother maybe. I'll ask him. Hold on."

Stephanie waited anxiously while Gwenith talked to her brother. She was back in a moment. "What did he say?" Stephanie asked eagerly.

"He's got a new comic book. He's going to stay home and read it this afternoon."

"Oh. Well, okay," Stephanie said. "No problem. I'll find a partner for Allie. You meet us at the public courts near the playground in an hour."

"I don't have a ride," Gwenith said.

"So walk," Stephanie told her. "Or better yet, jog. It's a great way to start our training program."

"You want me to *walk?*" Gwenith sounded shocked. "It's got to be at least ten blocks!"

"Okay, listen," Stephanie said. "Allie and I will stop by your house and get you. We'll be there soon."

Stephanie hung up and turned to Allie. "There's still hope," she cried. "Gwenith will do it. We're meeting her in a little while." Stephanie hurried down the stairs.

"Stephanie, I think you're forgetting something," Allie said, following her into the kitchen.

"What? Oh, right, we need a fourth player," Stephanie replied.

"No. I'm afraid there's another problem," Allie said.

"Oh, no, Allie," Stephanie moaned. "I can't take any more problems. What is it now?"

"You're supposed to be baby-sitting, remember?"

Stephanie gasped. "Oh, no! I can't leave the house! But I've just got to practice today! Allie, what am I going to do?"

Just then there was a thump and a shout from the living room, and a red ball rolled into the kitchen.

Stephanie stopped the ball with her foot. She stared down at it for a second. A grin spread across her face. "I've got it!" she cried.

"What?" Allie asked.

Michelle ran into the kitchen with the twins right behind her. "Steph, I need that ball back!" Michelle cried.

"You're not supposed to play ball in the house, guys," Stephanie scolded them.

Michelle and the twins looked sadly at Stephanie.

"But I've got an idea," Stephanie said. "After lunch we'll all go down to the tennis courts. And I'll teach you how to play tennis. How does that sound?"

The twins cheered and Michelle's face lit up. "I played tennis once with D.J.," Michelle said.

"Great," Stephanie said. "We need experienced players." She flashed Allie a big smile. "See?" Stephanie asked Allie. "I told you I'd find you a partner. And I just found *three!*"

CHAPTER
11

◆ ◢ ◣ ◆

"This will get me big points with Becky," Stephanie told Allie. "She loves it when I take the twins out to play."

Allie grinned. "Then your plan works for everyone."

They had reached Gwenith's house. Stephanie rang the bell and Gwenith opened the door.

"I'm ready!" Gwenith said. She glanced at the driveway and frowned. "Where's your dad's car? Who's driving us to the park?"

"We're walking, Gwenith," Stephanie said. "It's good exercise. Got to warm up those muscles before you play."

Gwenith looked doubtful. "I was going to save my energy for the courts," she said.

"Walking will give you energy," Stephanie told her. "Okay, everyone. Let's jog!"

Halfway down the block, Stephanie noticed that Gwenith was lagging behind Michelle. And the twins were even farther back. Then Alex stopped to examine a caterpillar on the sidewalk.

"Um, Allie, maybe you and I should give the twins piggyback rides to the park," she suggested.

Allie nodded and hoisted Nicky up onto her back. Stephanie gave Alex a ride. *But who's going to carry Gwenith?* she wondered.

Just then Stephanie heard a ringing noise in the distance. It was probably a car alarm. But it gave her an idea.

"Hey, that sounds like the ice cream truck," she called.

"Where?" Michelle asked, looking ahead. "I don't see an ice cream truck."

"Me either," Gwenith said.

Stephanie and Allie exchanged a knowing look. Trying to keep a straight face, Stephanie said, "Let's run over to the park. Maybe we can catch it. Come on, you guys!"

They all took off. It was hard work, running with Alex on her back. But it was worth it, Stephanie thought. Gwenith *was* trying to move faster. Still, she was the last one to reach the park.

"There's no ice cream truck!" Alex wailed.

"Where did it go?" Nicky asked.

"I guess we missed it," Stephanie said. "But I promise I'll get you ice cream on the way home."

The twins' faces lit up. "Okay," they said.

Gwenith sighed. "I really could have used an ice cream now," she said. She pulled out her racket and got ready to play.

Stephanie nudged Allie. "I guess that was a mean trick," she whispered. "But at least I got Gwenith to the park faster."

Stephanie clapped her hands and gathered everyone around her. "Okay, everybody. Here's the plan. Gwenith and I will play against Allie and the rest of you. And just for today, there are no rules. That means you're allowed to do *anything* to return the ball."

Michelle looked surprised. "Anything? You mean I can even catch it or kick it?"

"Yup," Stephanie replied. "Gwenith needs all the practice she can get." She turned to the twins. "Alex and Nicky, you guys chase any balls that Michelle and Allie miss. Okay?"

"Sure!" Nicky said. Alex nodded.

Michelle shrugged. "Whatever you say." She took her racket and stood next to Allie. Alex and Nicky stood behind them.

Stephanie served. Allie missed Stephanie's serve and the ball bounced toward Michelle.

"Got it!" Michelle cried. She swung her racket, but missed.

"I'll get it!" Alex chased the ball. He scooped it up in his hands.

"Throw it to me, Alex," Michelle called.

Alex tossed the ball to Michelle. Michelle caught it and threw it over the net as hard as she could.

"Yours!" Stephanie yelled at Gwenith. "Move!"

Gwenith stared at the ball but didn't move. It bounced once at Gwenith's feet. "Oops!" Gwenith blinked.

Stephanie groaned. "Time out!" she called. She jogged over to Gwenith. "Listen, Gwenith, this is our strategy—you will always play the net. Don't worry about the back of the court. I'll cover that. Okay?"

"Oh! I get it," Gwenith said. Her eyes lit up. "That way, I won't get confused, waiting to see where the ball will land. I have to hit only the balls that come near the net!"

"Yes!" Stephanie high-fived her. "But you have to move faster. Let's try it again."

"Hey—Allie and I can have a strategy too," Michelle said. "I'm not very good at tennis yet, but I *do* know how to play softball. Serve to me, Stephanie!"

Stephanie served. Michelle swung her racket as if it were a baseball bat. She whacked the ball back over the net.

"Nice hit!" Allie called.

This time Gwenith was ready. She swung her racket back and returned the ball. It zoomed over the net and Allie returned it to Stephanie. Stephanie sent it flying back to Allie.

"Way to go!" Stephanie cheered.

Allie missed the ball, but the twins chased after it. Nicky grabbed it and threw it to Michelle. Michelle whacked it over the net to Gwenith.

"It's a crazy system, but it works!" Stephanie said.

"Hey, this isn't so bad!" Gwenith replied. "It's fun!"

They kept up a long rally. "Looking good, Gwen!" Stephanie told her. "By the time we're done, you'll be a total tennis machine!"

Gwenith blushed, but Stephanie noticed that she tried even harder. Soon she was hitting almost every ball that came her way.

"Time out!" Stephanie finally called. "I think we all need a break."

Gwenith flung herself onto the grass under a

shady tree. "Whew! What a workout!" She groaned.

Allie, Michelle, and the twins sat on the grass too. "I'm pooped," Nicky said.

"But you're all doing great," Stephanie told them. She turned to Allie and lowered her voice. "Gwenith is really getting some confidence," she said. "She even worked up a sweat."

"She is getting better," Allie agreed. "But—"

"I know! But you and Michelle aren't nearly as good as Sara and Darcy," Stephanie finished for her. "Gwenith needs a much better team to play against."

Allie frowned. "That's *not* what I was going to say! Boy, Steph, you're getting as bad as Darcy. All you can think about is tennis, tennis, tennis!"

"Sorry," Stephanie mumbled. "But I really want Gwenith to play her best. You're doing your best today," she told Allie.

Allie smiled. "Thanks, Steph." She paused. "Can you really improve Gwenith's game in a week?"

Stephanie shrugged. "I don't know. But I'm going to try."

Stephanie stood up. "Let's play one more set," she said. "Then we'll all go for ice cream."

Gwenith groaned, but she climbed to her feet.

"Okay, one more set," she said. "But I'm getting a banana split to reward myself for this."

"What did you do to the twins, Stephanie?" Becky asked that evening. "They were asleep before I turned out the light!"

It was after dinner. The family was in the living room.

Michelle yawned. "Sleep sounds like fun," she mumbled. "Think I'll go to bed. Good night, everyone."

Michelle kissed everyone good night and went upstairs.

"I'm tired too," Stephanie agreed. "But I'm too worried to sleep."

"Worried about what, honey?" Danny asked.

"Well, it's a long story," Stephanie said.

"That's what families are for," Jesse told her.

So Stephanie explained about the challenge match with Darcy and Sara. And about her idea for a training program for Gwenith.

"But why do you have to train so hard, Stephanie?" Danny asked. "Aren't you playing this week with the Girls Tennis Club?"

"Yes, but it's not enough!" Stephanie replied. "Sara is brutally good at tennis."

"Well, what about Darcy? Is she a better player than you too?" Jesse asked.

"Yeah," Stephanie admitted. "And everybody is better than Gwenith. Way better."

"Sounds like you've got a real problem," Danny said.

"Yeah, looks like you really did it this time," Joey added.

"I know," Stephanie said. "Now Gwenith and I need to find a team to play against us every day until Saturday. It's impossible!"

"Well, I could play tonight," Becky offered. "I was going to use my exercise bike. But I'd much rather play tennis."

"I could play tomorrow night," Jesse said.

"And I can be Becky's partner tonight," Danny added. "Don't forget, I used to play tennis in college."

Stephanie sat up on the couch. Suddenly she wasn't feeling so discouraged. "You guys are the best!" she cried. "You mean you wouldn't mind playing with us?"

"Of course not," Danny said. "What about you, Joey? You used to play every day in college."

"Right!" Joey told Stephanie. "They used to call me the human lobster. I could lob the ball into the clouds."

"No, Joey, they called you that when you played in the sun too long," Danny pointed out. "You were as red as a lobster!"

Everyone laughed.

"Still, I'd be glad to knock a few balls around with you, Stephanie," Joey said. "I'll play tomorrow as Jesse's partner. And I'll play another night, too, if you need me."

"Me too," Danny added. Becky and Jesse nodded also.

Stephanie jumped off the couch. "This is great!" she said. "I'll call Gwenith right now and tell her the good news." She headed for the phone, then stopped and turned around.

"Thanks a whole lot, all of you. With a little help from Team Tanner, we might just pull this off!"

CHAPTER
12

♦ ◀ ▸ ♦

"Hey, Steph!" Allie slid her lunch tray onto the table. She sat down next to Stephanie. "Sorry I'm late. I had to come all the way from the music rooms on the other side of the building."

"What were you doing there?" Stephanie asked.

"Practicing with this guy in my guitar class. We got a pass from study hall."

"Is he cute?" Stephanie asked.

"No, but he's a great guitar player," Allie said. She took a huge bite out of her sandwich. "I'm starved."

Stephanie stared at her own lunch. Suddenly, she didn't have much of an appetite. She was nervous about eating lunch with Darcy.

"Allie, did you talk to Darcy yet today?" she asked.

"No," Allie answered. "In fact, we didn't talk at all over the weekend. I kind of miss her."

"Yeah, me too," Stephanie said.

"Well, what did you expect? You're the one who challenged her to the big tennis match," Allie pointed out. She sighed. "It felt really weird not to have one three-way phone call all weekend."

"I know. It's really like Sara and Darcy are best friends now," Stephanie replied. She swallowed over a big lump in her throat. "Darcy didn't even show up at the pay phone this morning."

"Well, at least lunch will be normal. The three of us together, right?" Allie asked.

"Uh, hi, guys! How are you doing?"

Stephanie looked up. Darcy was standing at their table, holding her lunch tray. Stephanie stared at her. Darcy flushed.

It doesn't feel like things are "normal" again, Stephanie thought.

Allie smiled brightly. "Darcy! It's good to see you! We missed you at the pay phone this morning," she said.

"Well, I had to meet with Sara," Darcy answered. "To discuss our doubles strategy."

"Really?" Stephanie raised an eyebrow. "That's a surprise. Gwenith and I already have our strategy worked out."

"So do we," Darcy replied. "We're just making it better."

Allie cleared her throat. "Uh, what did you get for lunch today, Darce?" she asked, trying to change the subject.

"Spaghetti," Darcy answered. "I'm carbo-loading for extra energy. Not that I need extra energy. Sara and I have enough energy to win a match right now," she bragged.

"Oh, yeah? Well, Gwenith and I—" Stephanie began to say.

"Come on, you two," Allie interrupted. "Don't be like this, guys. We're all best friends, right?"

"Stephanie started it. She's the one who challenged us," Darcy said. She gave Allie an angry look. "I don't know why you're taking her side!"

"I'm not!" Allie protested.

"Oh! Then are you on Darcy's side?" Stephanie demanded.

"No!" Allie cried. "I—"

"Well, I don't care whose side anyone's on!" Darcy exclaimed.

She dropped her tray onto the table. "I'm not hungry anymore," she said. "I think I'll go find

Sara. Maybe we'll skip lunch and get in some extra practice. So we can really destroy you on Saturday!" Darcy stormed off.

"Can you believe that?" Stephanie cried. "She is completely out of control!"

"Ummm, Stephanie," Allie said. "I think you might be forgetting something. You were a little out of control yourself, remember?"

"Only because Darcy was so obnoxious, and—" Stephanie stopped talking as Maggie Shapiro approached the table.

"Hey, Stephanie. I heard about the big match on Saturday," Maggie said. "Do you really think you and Gwenith can beat Sara and Darcy?"

Stephanie stared at Maggie in surprise. "Who told you about the match?" she asked.

"Sara did," Maggie said. "Her locker is right next to mine. And she said you and Gwenith don't have a chance of beating them."

"Well, Sara doesn't know what she's talking about," Stephanie insisted. "Gwenith and I are going to blow them away!"

Maggie grinned. "Cool! I can't wait to see this match," she said.

"You won't be disappointed," Stephanie told her. "Tell everyone in the club!"

As Maggie walked away, Allie shook her head.

"Steph, you just invited the whole club to come watch your challenge match."

"I know," Stephanie said. "But I can't stand it that Sara is bragging all over school."

"Stephanie, are you sure it's worth all this trouble?" Allie asked. "I mean, you joined the Girls Tennis Club to have fun—not to hold a grudge match against your best friend!"

"Well, I can't back out now," Stephanie told her.

Allie sighed. "You're going to kill yourself with all this extra tennis practice."

"It won't be that bad," Stephanie insisted. "Sunday was a breeze! We just did weight training and jumping rope and jogging. And by the end of the day, Gwenith was really getting into it."

"Stephanie, help!" Gwenith's voice broke into the conversation. She threw herself into the seat across from Stephanie.

"I can't believe what's happening!" Gwenith moaned. "Everybody in school knows about the match on Saturday! We're going to look so bad."

"*Everybody* in school?" Stephanie swallowed hard.

Gwenith nodded. "Yeah, and they also know that Sara was team captain at her old school. Nobody thinks we can win!"

"Don't worry," Stephanie said. "This just means that you and I have to train harder than we thought."

Stephanie pulled out a notebook and gazed at their practice schedule.

"Tonight we play against Uncle Jesse and Joey," she told Gwenith. "Then we work out with weights. Then watch a tennis video. Okay?"

"But what about my science homework?" Gwenith said, biting her lip.

"Gwenith, you have to set some priorities if you want to be an athlete," Stephanie said firmly. "Maybe you can get an extension on your homework. Or come up with a really good excuse for why you didn't do it. You've got to take each problem as it comes and deal with it. That's what competitive sports are all about!"

"Stephanie!" Allie said. "Hello? Aren't you the one who said that Darcy was out of control? Don't you think you're taking this competition a little too seriously? It's only a game."

"Only a game!" Stephanie repeated, amazed. "How can you say that, Allie? You saw how Darcy acted just now. This is serious. What's the point of playing if we don't play to win? Right, Gwenith?"

Gwenith looked frightened. "Uh, right," she said.

Stephanie turned to Allie with a smile. "See?" She threw an arm around Gwenith's shoulders. "By the end of this week, Gwenith and I will *definitely* be the winning team!"

CHAPTER

13

◆ ◀ ◆ ◆

"Yeah, Gwen! Way to go!" Stephanie shouted. It was Friday evening—and Team Tanner's final practice before the big match.

The week had flown by. Every spare minute of the afternoon and evening was crammed full of tennis practice or working out. Stephanie and Gwenith had played against Team Tanner every single day. They had lifted weights and jogged until they had no more strength left. Then they watched tennis videos and read about team strategy.

And they had finally won their first game!

"I can't believe it! We really beat Joey and Jesse!" Gwenith beamed. "We actually won a match!"

Stephanie slapped Gwenith a high-five. "See what a little training can do?"

"A little?" Gwenith exclaimed. "I'm practically a different person! I don't get out of breath anymore. I hardly ever hit balls out of bounds. I don't even hit into the net very much!"

"True," Stephanie said. "We played hard, and we beat the competition!"

"Hey, Team Tanner played hard too," Jesse reminded her. "This week got the whole family back in shape, not just you and Gwenith," he said. "And tonight's game was the toughest one yet. Too bad we lost, Joey old pal." Jesse slapped Joey on the back.

"Yeah, well, don't rub it in," Joey complained. "You nearly whacked me with your racket in that last set."

"Boy, was your face red when you lost the point," Jesse teased Joey. "Now I *really* know why they called you the human lobster in college!"

"Well, I wouldn't have lost. But the sun was in my eyes," Joey protested. "I never saw the ball coming at me."

"Not until it almost took your nose off." Stephanie giggled. "Anyway, I'm so excited that we won!"

Stephanie threw herself down on the grass beside the tennis court. Gwenith collapsed next to her.

"Winning was great. But now I need dinner!" She groaned. "I'm starving after that workout."

"The workout isn't over yet," Stephanie told her. "We're jogging home from the park, remember?"

"We can drive you," Jesse offered.

Gwenith sighed. "Thanks, but Stephanie is right. We should jog."

"Okay," Joey said. "We'll have your super-duper high-carb pasta dinner ready when you get to the house."

"Great!" Stephanie said. "See you guys later!" She waved good-bye. "Come on, Gwenith." She pulled Gwenith to her feet.

They made it home in record time. They were so hungry that they both ate two helpings of dinner. Afterward, they watched the tennis video twice. They really studied the strategy of the professional players. Finally it was time for Gwenith to head home. She gathered her tennis things together. She paused at the front door.

"I can't believe the big match is tomorrow," Gwenith said. She bit her lip nervously. "Kids I don't even know have been wishing me luck. Half the school is going to be there. I hope we don't look totally dumb."

"We won't," Stephanie assured her. "We are an incredible team. Just remember how we won tonight. And remember our strategy!"

"I will," Gwenith said.

"And don't forget to stretch your muscles after you get home tonight," Stephanie instructed. "And go to bed early."

"Okay, okay," Gwenith said. "See you tomorrow morning—at the match."

Gwenith left.

We will win tomorrow. We can—and we will! Stephanie told herself.

She yawned. *Whew! I'm ready for a good night's sleep myself,* she thought. She glanced at her watch. There was just enough time for a quick call to Allie. She dialed the living room phone.

"It's me!" Stephanie said when Allie answered. "Gwenith just left. And guess what? We beat the pants off Jesse and Joey tonight! I'm totally psyched about playing tomorrow."

"Well, good luck," Allie told her. She hesitated. "Don't feel bad, Steph, but I think I should call Darcy and wish her good luck too."

"Oh." Stephanie was silent for a moment.

"Steph?" Allie asked. "Don't you miss talking to Darcy? I mean, it was weird for me all week. I felt

112

like a rat no matter who I talked to. Sometimes I felt like I couldn't be friends with you *or* Darcy."

Stephanie didn't answer. She had to admit, it had been a strange week.

"I don't know what to say," she finally told Allie. "I guess it has been sort of weird. Especially at tennis club. Not that I *wanted* to talk to Darcy—especially not with Sara around. But it sure felt strange not meeting Darcy at the pay phone every morning. And eating lunch without her every day." Stephanie frowned. There was a funny feeling in the pit of her stomach.

Probably just nerves about the match tomorrow, she told herself.

"I wish this whole thing had never happened," Allie said. "I can't stand having my two best friends not talking to each other." Allie sighed. "But I guess it will all be over tomorrow. And then things can go back to normal, right?"

"Right," Stephanie answered. But for the first time, a new thought struck her.

"Allie," Stephanie said slowly, "what *will* happen after tomorrow? I mean, if Darcy and Sara win, I don't know how I'll feel about it."

"Yeah, and what will Darcy do if you and Gwenith win?" Allie asked.

The funny feeling in the pit of Stephanie's stomach got worse. All week she had thought only about winning the match. But now she wondered if she and Darcy would ever be friends again.

"Well, anyway, good luck," Allie said. "See you at the courts tomorrow."

"Yeah. See you." Stephanie hung up the phone.

Well, there's no time to worry about it now, she told herself. *The most important thing is for me to get to sleep!*

Stephanie hurried upstairs and flung open her bedroom door.

"Michelle! What are you doing in here?' Stephanie exclaimed.

Michelle was sprawled on her own bed. Four stuffed animals were snuggled in her arms.

"I couldn't fall asleep in D.J.'s room last night," Michelle explained. "So I came in here for some of my stuffed animals. I figured they would help me sleep better."

"Okay, but you have to leave now," Stephanie told her. "I've got my big tennis match tomorrow. I need every minute of sleep I can get! So go to D.J.'s room, okay?"

"Okay," Michelle said.

Stephanie closed the door, changed into her pajamas, and climbed into bed. Her arms and legs felt as if they were made of wood, they were so stiff and heavy. She pulled the blankets up under her chin. Suddenly Michelle threw the door open again.

Stephanie groaned. "What is it now?" she asked.

"I need my pillow," Michelle answered. "I can't sleep without it."

"So, get it. And close the door on your way out," Stephanie muttered.

Michelle grabbed the pillow from her bed and went back to D.J.'s room. Stephanie lay in bed, staring at the ceiling. Light from the street shone through her window, making strange shadow shapes.

Stephanie sighed and turned over onto her side. *I just have to get some sleep!*

She closed her eyes and felt herself drifting off. Suddenly the light overhead clicked on, jolting her awake. She sat up and rubbed her eyes. Michelle was back in the room, carrying an armful of stuffed animals.

"I still can't sleep!" Michelle wailed.

"Well, I can!" Stephanie replied. "But you keep waking me up. What is your problem?"

Michelle dumped her animals on the bed. "D.J.'s room is no fun."

"Sleeping isn't supposed to be fun," Stephanie grumbled.

"Can't I come back and sleep in this room with you?" Michelle asked.

Stephanie sat up. "But what about the phone?" she asked.

"I don't need it anymore," Michelle answered. "Now that Mandy named her gerbil, we don't have anything important to talk about anymore."

Stephanie was suddenly wide awake. "Michelle, I let you use that room so you could have the phone to yourself. Do you mean it sat there all week without being used?"

Michelle nodded. She put her pillow back in its place and arranged her stuffed animals on her bed along the wall. Then she climbed into her bed.

"I can't believe this!" Stephanie said, shaking her head. "Well, if we're not going to use D.J.'s room, we should at least use her phone."

Stephanie rolled out of bed and stomped into D.J.'s room. She picked up the phone and carried it across the hall and into her room. She placed it on her dresser.

"There," Stephanie said. "Now we're both happy."

Michelle smiled. "Even D.J. will be happy, because I'm not messing up her room."

"Right," Stephanie said. "Now go to bed, Michelle. I have the biggest tennis game of my life tomorrow. And I'll never win if I don't get some sleep!"

CHAPTER
14

◆ ◀ ▶ ◆

"Well, um, good luck," Darcy said. She stuck out her hand toward Stephanie.

Stephanie hesitated. This was so weird! She was about to try to destroy her ex–best friend at tennis.

It was early Saturday morning. Stephanie had driven to the school courts with her dad, Jesse, Joey, and Michelle. Becky had decided to stay home with the twins.

They stopped to pick up Gwenith on the way. She and Stephanie hadn't said much in the car. Stephanie still found it hard to believe that the match was actually happening. But she believed it when they got to school. The bleachers were packed with kids.

Most of the Girls Tennis Club members had

shown up. And a whole bunch of other kids were there too. Stephanie felt as if everyone were watching to see if she would shake Darcy's hand. Stephanie wiped her palms off on her skirt.

Smile, Stephanie told herself. *Don't let anybody see how scared you are! Especially not Darcy!*

She took a deep breath and forced herself to look Darcy straight in the eye. "Good luck," she muttered. She took Darcy's hand and shook it.

What is she thinking? Stephanie wondered.

There wasn't any special expression on Darcy's face. Stephanie couldn't tell if Darcy was nervous and hiding it, like she was. *Or maybe she's really sure that she and Sara will beat us,* Stephanie thought.

She had already noticed that Darcy was wearing her new green pleated tennis skirt, the one that matched Sara's.

Gwenith and Stephanie had decided to dress alike also. They were both wearing white shorts and bright blue T-shirts.

Just then Gwenith came up to her. "Ready?" she asked. "I think Sara is about to announce the match."

"Ready," Stephanie answered.

Well, this is it, Darcy is going to try to beat me, Stephanie told herself. *So, I'm going to try just as hard to beat Darcy!*

They took their positions on the court. Stephanie and Gwenith faced Darcy and Sara.

"Okay, everyone! Quiet down!" Sara called. "This is a challenge match. We'll play by standard rules. Best two sets out of three wins the match. Maggie Shapiro will be the referee." Sara nodded at Maggie, who stood on the sidelines.

Stephanie glanced into the stands. Her family was sitting in the top row. Danny wore a wide-brimmed hat to protect his face from the sun. Stephanie caught his eye and Danny lifted the hat and waved it at her. Joey, Jesse, and Michelle shot her thumbs-up signs.

"Okay, people, let's go!" Maggie said. She nodded at Sara.

Sara approached the net with her racket. She spun it. Stephanie called "heads" and won the serve.

"I'll serve," Stephanie told Gwenith.

Gwenith looked really nervous. She shifted from one foot to the other and bit both her lips. Stephanie had butterflies in her own stomach. But she was determined not to let it bother her.

"Relax, Gwenith," she said. "Remember Team Tanner! Just play the net! We can do it!"

Stephanie took one last deep breath. Then she tossed the ball high into the air. She swung her racket and sent it sailing across the net. The match was on!

Stephanie soon forgot about the crowd of people watching. For the first time, she really was focused on the ball. Nothing escaped her. She was really concentrating. And it helped. All she could think of was returning every single shot. She had never played better.

Sara delivered one of her wicked line drives. It flew past Stephanie—and past Gwenith. Gwenith lunged after it, but missed. She gasped and turned pale.

"No problem, Gwenith. That ball was out!" Stephanie shouted.

"I'm sure it was in," Sara replied. They both turned to look at Maggie.

"It was out!" Maggie decided.

Sara frowned. "Maggie, I know more about the rules than you do—" she began.

"That ball was out!" Danny shouted from the bleachers.

"Way to go, Steph and Gwenith!" Joey added. Some kids in the crowd applauded.

Sara scowled. "We don't need the point anyway," she told Maggie. "Let them have it." She flounced back to her side of the court.

"I'm so sorry," Gwenith said to Stephanie.

Stephanie narrowed her eyes. "It *was* out," she told Gwenith. "And Sara just made me even madder than I was."

Stephanie was more determined to win than ever. Still, Sara and Darcy won the first set. As they switched sides, Stephanie huddled with Gwenith.

"Don't worry," Stephanie told her. "We're playing our best. You're doing great, and you're not even out of breath yet."

"I'm really trying," Gwenith answered.

Stephanie clapped her on the shoulder. "We can do it. The next set is ours!" she cried.

This time Gwenith served. Stephanie held her breath—but the ball sailed easily over the net.

"Yes!" Stephanie shouted. She noticed that Darcy and Sara seemed surprised that Gwenith had gotten off such a good serve. Sara faltered, but recovered in time to return the ball with her usual killer speed. Somehow, Stephanie slammed it back to her.

They rallied for a while in total silence. Sara returned one to Gwenith. Gwenith rushed the net and shot the ball toward Darcy. Darcy missed the ball.

"Yes!" Stephanie cried again.

"Darcy! Wake up!" Sara yelled. Across the court, Stephanie saw Darcy frown.

"I can't believe I did that!" Gwenith said. She seemed even more surprised than Darcy had been.

Stephanie clapped Gwenith on the back. "Our point! Way to go, Gwen!" she shouted. She could hear her family cheering in the bleachers.

On the next serve, the ball flew toward Darcy again.

"Watch your footing!" Sara yelled to her.

"What?" Darcy turned to look at Sara just as the ball went whizzing by. It bounced into the bleachers. Stephanie and Gwenith won another point— and the second set!

Stephanie and Gwenith slapped a high-five and hugged each other. "This just keeps getting better!" Gwenith said in amazement.

Across the court, Sara angrily stomped her foot on the ground. "What is your problem?" she yelled at Darcy. "We should have won this set!"

"Sorry," Darcy murmured. Stephanie saw her cheeks darken in embarrassment.

"Well, pay attention," Sara scolded her. "This is the third set. Now we're tied. We could actually lose this match!"

"I'm doing my best," Darcy snapped back.

"Well, do better. And watch your grip. It's really off," Sara said. "Try to remember what I told you about *everything!*"

Stephanie had never seen Darcy look so angry. The game continued, but this time Sara was chasing after every ball. She was returning most of them without even giving Darcy a chance.

"Sara looks tired," Gwenith muttered to Stephanie.

"Who wouldn't be?" Stephanie answered. "She's practically playing the whole game alone. Poor Darcy," she added.

"Well, we're playing like a perfect team," Gwenith replied.

Stephanie grinned. It was true. Their doubles strategy was working. She and Gwenith returned every ball that flew their way. Meanwhile, Sara looked more and more frantic. Darcy just looked angry.

Halfway through the third set, Stephanie and Gwenith had the advantage. Then it was Darcy's turn to serve.

"Now, remember, concentrate," Sara warned her partner.

"I am concentrating," Darcy growled back. She took a deep breath, tossed the ball high, and smashed her racket at it. The ball slammed into the net.

"Nooo!" Sara groaned. "What are you doing?"

Darcy turned and glared at her. "I'm serving the ball, okay?"

"Well, serve it *right!*" Sara snapped.

"I don't believe this," Gwenith whispered to Stephanie. "Their game is totally falling apart!"

Stephanie couldn't believe it either. "If Darcy blows this serve, we'll actually win the match!" Stephanie faced the net again. She gripped her racket tightly.

With a determined expression, Darcy got ready to serve. She tossed the ball in the air and brought her racket down—sending the ball into the net again!

"Game, set, match to Stephanie and Gwenith!" Maggie shouted.

A roar went up from the bleachers where Stephanie's family was sitting.

"Yes!" Gwenith shouted. "We did it! We really did it! We beat them!"

Gwenith threw her arms around Stephanie and squeezed. Stephanie was stunned. "We really did it," she murmured.

"Well, you said we could do it," Gwenith reminded her.

"I know," Stephanie replied. "But I never really believed it!"

Gwenith stared at her for a minute. Then she and Stephanie both burst out laughing. "What do we do now?" Gwenith asked.

"Shake the opponents' hands," Stephanie said. She and Gwenith approached the net.

"Great game," Sara said. Her voice was tight, but she didn't seem angry at them. She shook both their hands.

I guess when you compete against real talent like us, you don't mind losing, Stephanie thought.

Then Darcy stepped up. "Congratulations, Stephanie," Darcy said quietly. "You played an awesome match. You too, Gwenith."

"Thanks, Darce, I—" Stephanie began.

Darcy dropped her eyes away from Stephanie's gaze. She turned and began to walk away. Stephanie watched her go.

"Come on, Stephanie," Gwenith interrupted. "I'll buy you the biggest banana split you ever had. You deserve it. In fact, we both do!"

Her stomach rumbled loudly and Gwenith laughed. "I was too nervous to eat breakfast this morning. But now I feel empty inside."

"Thanks, Gwen. Maybe some other time," Stephanie told her. "I mean, I feel kind of empty inside too. But it's the kind of empty that even a banana split can't fix."

Stephanie gazed after Darcy. Suddenly, winning didn't seem so great anymore.

CHAPTER
15

◆ ◀ ▶ ◆

Stephanie dropped her tennis racket by the front door. She shuffled into the kitchen. Danny, Jesse, Joey, and Michelle followed her. Jesse went straight to the refrigerator and pulled out a carton of ice cream. "Sundaes all around," he announced.

"None for me, Uncle Jesse," Stephanie told him. She poured herself a glass of water.

Becky was in the kitchen, getting an early start on dinner. She gazed at Stephanie in concern. "Hey! You look beat," she said. "But cheer up. You know what they say, Steph. It's not whether you win or lose, it's—"

"But, Aunt Becky, we won," Stephanie interrupted.

"You should have seen her," Danny said. He

beamed with pride. "Stephanie and Gwenith were great!"

"They were awesome," Michelle told Becky.

Becky gazed at Stephanie in amazement. "You won?" she asked.

"Don't you have any faith?' Joey said. "After all our training? Of course she won!"

Becky frowned in confusion. "Then why the long face, Stephanie?" she asked.

Stephanie sighed. "I won the match," she said. "But I lost my best friend. Darcy couldn't even look at me afterward."

Danny knelt down by Stephanie's chair. "Steph, you lost a tennis game. Not a friendship," he told her.

"You don't know, Dad," Stephanie said. "Darcy and I haven't been friends for nearly two weeks!" Stephanie moaned. "Allie was right. I should never have taken this tennis thing so seriously."

"Aren't you being a little hard on yourself?" Danny asked.

"I don't know." Stephanie shrugged. "I don't even know why I was so mad at Darcy. So, she wanted to play tennis with Sara. So what? Friends don't have to do *everything* together, right?"

"Well, right," Danny said.

"I guess I *was* jealous," Stephanie muttered. She

127

stared glumly at her glass of water. "Hey, that's it!" she suddenly shouted. "That's what Allie was trying to tell me! Boy, I really *do* owe Darcy an apology. And Allie too! This really *was* all my fault!" Stephanie jumped up and gave Danny a big hug and a kiss.

"Thanks, Dad!" she cried.

"Thanks for what?" Danny looked totally confused.

"I'll explain later," Stephanie told him. "Right now I've got to make a *very* important phone call!"

Stephanie ran into the living room. *For once, I beat Michelle to the phone!* she thought. *Thank goodness!* She dialed Allie's number. Just then the doorbell rang.

Stephanie groaned. "Who could *that* be?" She hung up the phone and flung open the door.

"Allie! I was just calling you! You have to make a three-way phone call. I have to tell Darcy—" Stephanie stopped talking as Allie pulled Darcy through the front door.

Stephanie gasped. "What—?"

Darcy looked at Stephanie and then at the front door, as if she wanted to make a run for it.

"I was going to call you," Stephanie said. "That is, I was going to call Allie to make a three-way phone call to you."

"You were?" Darcy asked in surprise.

Stephanie nodded. She had so much to say, she didn't know where to begin. But just as she opened her mouth to apologize, the phone rang. Michelle burst through the kitchen door.

"It's for me!" she yelled, running for the phone. "Mandy just got another new gerbil!"

Stephanie rolled her eyes. "Some habits never die," she grumbled.

Michelle spoke into the telephone. "It's for you," she told Stephanie in disappointment. "It's Sara Albright."

"Sara?" Stephanie asked. "Why is she calling here?"

Darcy looked embarrassed. "Maybe she's looking for me," Darcy said. "My mom probably told her I'm over here." Darcy sighed and took the phone from Michelle. "Hello, Sara—" she began. Then she frowned. "Stephanie?" she said. "Uh, sure, she's right here." Darcy handed the phone to Stephanie.

"For me?" Stephanie took the receiver and said, "Hello?"

"Stephanie, hi. It's Sara. I wanted to tell you again what a great match you played today."

"Oh, thanks," Stephanie said. "So what's up?"

"Well, I was wondering . . ." Sara hesitated.

"Maybe you'd like to be my doubles partner. It could really be fun."

"What? But what about Darcy?" Stephanie blurted out. "She's already your partner."

"She *was* my partner," Sara replied. "But you turned out to be a better player. Darcy got totally rattled today. But you were excellent under pressure. That counts a lot."

"Thanks, I think," Stephanie said.

"We could be a really cool team," Sara continued. "I bet we could beat everybody in the club. What do you think?"

Stephanie frowned. "Sara, you're a really good player, and we might play together sometime. But I would never do that to Darcy. She's still my best friend."

"Oh," Sara said. "Are you sure?"

"Positive," Stephanie answered. "I don't want to be your partner."

Stephanie hung up and turned to her friends. Allie and Darcy stared at her.

"Did we hear what I think we heard?" Darcy demanded. "Did Sara just ask you to be her tennis partner?"

"Yup," Stephanie said.

Darcy seemed stunned for a moment. "I can't believe she would do something like that."

"Believe it," Stephanie said. "I think Sara cares about only one thing. And that's winning."

"She sure doesn't care how she treats other people," Allie remarked.

Stephanie looked at Darcy. "Well, I got carried away too. All I could think about was beating you and Sara. That's why I wanted to call you, Darcy. I feel so bad about everything."

"I'm the one who should apologize," Darcy replied. "I can't believe I was ever so impressed by Sara."

"Well, she really gets to you," Stephanie said. "I was so jealous of you and Sara. I was like some monster who would do anything to win. And then, when I *did* win, I felt like a total loser."

"You did?" Darcy asked.

"Yeah. Because I felt like I'd lost your friendship forever."

"Well, I should never have signed up to be her partner without talking to you first," Darcy replied. "That's not how friends treat each other. I'm really sorry, Stephanie."

"Well, we both learned our lesson," Stephanie said.

"Yeah. Because now I know how it feels to be dumped for someone else. Almost," Darcy teased. "Thanks for turning Sara down, Steph."

"That's okay," Stephanie said. "To be honest, I'm glad I played with Gwenith. She's really great. And I would never have known that if you hadn't decided to play with someone else."

"See?" Allie put in. "Sometimes it's good *not* to do everything with your best friends."

Darcy sat next to Stephanie on the couch. "Maybe you and Gwenith can teach me to improve, now that I stink at tennis."

"No way!" Stephanie cried. "Darcy, you're still a better player than I am. You just had a bad day. Sara really got to you, that's all."

"I'll say she did. She worked me pretty hard all week," Darcy admitted. "I guess I couldn't take the pressure."

"Well, the pressure is off now," Allie said. "So why don't we all celebrate. How about ordering some pizza? I'm starving."

"Sounds good to me," Stephanie said. "What do we want on it? Extra cheese and mushrooms?"

"I hate mushrooms," Darcy said. "How about extra cheese and pepperoni?"

"How about no pepperoni, regular cheese, and extra—" Stephanie began to argue.

"You guys!" Allie cried. "Stop it right now! Don't start fighting again. You just made up!"

Darcy and Stephanie looked at each other and

started laughing. Darcy threw a pillow at Stephanie, and Stephanie threw it back.

"I know!" Stephanie said. "Let's order a pizza with *everything* on it. Then we can take off what we don't like—and everybody will be happy."

"Good idea," Darcy agreed.

"So, now that our lunch is settled, and we're all friends again, what should we do later?" Allie asked. "What are you guys up for?"

"Just about anything is fine with me," Darcy said.

"Me too," Stephanie agreed.

She and Darcy and Allie looked at one another.

"As long as it isn't tennis!" they all said together.